"I don't like being taken for one of your—one of your..."

"My what?" His eyes glinted.

"Your methods of relaxation," she snapped. "Like the other... *ladies* who have slept in that sexy boudoir you call a cabin."

His deep laughter filled the room. "Are you trying to tell me you didn't enjoy giving that sultry treatment to Lance? The little smile, the starry eyes, all that beautiful body language? You had me convinced, too."

"I was only following your lead," Lacey said.

Jonathan held her gaze, his eyes darkening. "Keep following," he said as he pulled her close. His mouth came down on hers, gentle, warm, and seeking, and a traitorous impulse welled up inside her, making her want to respond, to yield completely.

Dear Reader:

Summer is here! And we've got six new SECOND CHANCE AT LOVE romances to add to your pleasure in the new season. So sit back, put your feet up, and enjoy . . .

You've also got a lot to look forward to in the months ahead—delightful romances from exciting new writers, as well as fabulous stories from your tried-and-true favorites. You know you can rely on SECOND CHANCE AT LOVE to provide the kind of satisfying romantic entertainment you expect.

We continue to receive and enjoy your letters—so please keep them coming! Remember: Your thoughts and feelings about SECOND CHANCE AT LOVE books are what enable us to publish the kind of romances you not only enjoy reading once, but also keep in a special place and read again and again.

Warm wishes for a beautiful summer,

Ellen Edwards

Ellen Edwards
SECOND CHANCE AT LOVE
The Berkley Publishing Group
200 Madison Avenue
New York, N.Y. 10016

Second Chance at Love

KISSES INCOGNITO
CHRISTA MERLIN

SECOND CHANCE AT LOVE
BOOK

KISSES INCOGNITO

Copyright © 1984 by Christa Merlin

All rights reserved. No part of this publication may be reproduced or transmitted in any form or by any means, electronic or mechanical, including photocopy, recording, or any information storage and retrieval system, without permission in writing from the publisher.

Requests for permission to make copies of any part of the work should be mailed to: Permissions, Second Chance at Love, The Berkley Publishing Group, 200 Madison Avenue, New York, NY 10016.

First edition published June 1984

First printing

"Second Chance at Love" and the butterfly emblem are trademarks belonging to Jove Publications, Inc.

Printed in the United States of America

Second Chance at Love books are published by
The Berkley Publishing Group
200 Madison Avenue, New York, NY 10016

KISSES INCOGNITO

Chapter 1

THE CANOE WAITED. Tied to an old dock where still, blue water mirrored a perfect replica below, the bright yellow shape beckoned toward adventure. Lacey Thomas stopped her small car to look, ruffling her blue-black cap of hair with slender, ink-stained fingers. After the noisy confusion of *The Clarion*'s newsroom, it would be wonderful to paddle out into the bay alone. Not that her job wasn't wonderful, too. She'd been lucky, a year ago, at the age of twenty-five, to find a job down here on a small-town newspaper; luckier still to discover a garage apartment behind an old waterfront house. Rental units on Florida's waterways were scarce and expensive, even in little Tarpon City.

Stretching with a sigh of pleasure, Lacey assessed the weather. She knew that afternoon squalls were dangerous, but today there wasn't a cloud in the sky. She would be safe on the wide bay. She drove on, past the big house, to park her car and run up the steps to her apartment. A gray cat, sleeping in one of the chairs, sat up and yawned widely, watching Lacey with slanted golden eyes as she flung down her purse and headed for the bedroom, stripping off her silk blouse as she went.

"Ready to go, Cabot?" She threw the question over her shoulder, and the cat jumped down to follow her, his long back legs and stump of tail proclaiming his Manx ancestry. Springing to the bed, he sat down to wait as she put on shorts, a thin knit pullover, and a pair of canvas shoes. As she headed for the door, he sprang from the bed to accompany her.

"Are you sure you want to join me today?" Lacey asked, laughing. "You might get wet again, you know." Cabot passed her going down the steps, and she was amused by his angry, laid-back ears, the irritated switch of his stump of tail.

"Why don't you teach the cat to paddle? That way, you'd have help." Her landlord, Bert Andrews, and his wife, Marie, were on the porch of the old house, identical grins on their wrinkled faces. Lacey smiled back at them and waved.

"He'd always be paddling toward home," she called, too excited to stop for a chat. Poor Cabot, she thought, watching him walk gingerly along the dock. He hated water, hated the canoe. But unless she shut him inside the apartment, he went where she went. And he was company—her one link with a past that had included, after all, some happy moments.

Sending the canoe along with short, sure strokes, hearing the whisper of water along the sides, Lacey felt her tension slip away. Cabot, crouched in the bow, sat up and looked over the side, his ears going flat again. She recalled him as a kitten, in the apartment in New York. A ball of gray fur, with a button of tail. A peace offering from Rick Lonigan, after one of their spectacular arguments. The only thing of value, she thought wryly, that had come from that relationship. Would she and Rick still be fighting if she hadn't left him? Probably. But her eyes, the same soft gray as Cabot's fur, were clouded for only a moment. She was through with Rick, through with any man who tried to make her into an image of his own desires. She stopped paddling and rested. The canoe slowed, began to drift with the quiet tide. A hundred feet away, a fisherman, stooped in his small boat, was pulling in a net dotted with small, shining fish. Lacey raised her paddle in greeting and he waved back.

"Got Cabot with you again?"

She nodded, smiling, and he laughed, as he continued

to pull methodically, the weights of his net sounding like stones dropping in his boat.

"You're famous," Lacey told the cat, and sat forward, beginning to paddle again toward a distant island. The days were long; she had time to gather clams and be home before dark. On the other side of the island, along the edge of Fisherman's Cove, there were hundreds of clams.

When she reached the island, she took off her shoes. On the flats, the tide was too high to see the clams winking. The murky water and the thought of crabs and sharp shells made wading less than fun. Still, she was here, and clam chowder made a great supper. Lacey slid over the side and began pulling the canoe along behind her as she waded, her bare feet cautiously feeling for solid shapes in the thick mud.

With a dozen large clams in the bottom of the canoe, she reached a point of land where mangroves thrust out long limbs, trailing rootlets down to fasten in the mud below. Lacey was careful to keep away from the overhanging branches, pushing her slim legs against the swirl of the tide as she passed them. Suddenly, she came to an abrupt halt. A flat-bottomed rowboat that had been hidden by the branches now swung directly in front of her, only a few feet away. And on the other side, with one large hand gripping the gunwale, stood the man from Fisherman's Cove. Her first impulse was to turn and run, an impossible feat in the thigh-deep water. She had never seen him before, but she had heard enough. The fishermen talked of his size, his temper. A drifter, they said, who holed up every year for months in an old, deserted house on the cove, coming and going secretively. Give him a wide berth, they told her. He's trouble. Lacey's hand trembled on the canoe.

"Excuse me," she said, and thought how stupidly breathless she sounded. But he was even bigger than she had imagined, and the heavy muscles on his wide, bronzed torso were impressive. Not that size frightened her, but his expression was anything but friendly. He was younger than she had expected him to be—thirty-four, perhaps. Beneath tousled brown hair his face was tense, the heavy brows drawn down over icy blue eyes, his jaw set so hard it bunched his flat cheeks. "I mean," she added faintly, "I won't bother you. I'll just go back the way I came..." She watched the cold blue eyes slide over her face, drop for an instant to the curves revealed by her damp, clinging pullover, then sweep up again to catch and hold her alarmed gaze. A warm jolt of something—a strange kind of recognition—shot through her, making her breathless again, then faded as he turned away abruptly.

"Unnecessary," he said in a deep, impersonal voice. "I'm leaving." He tossed a dripping clam into his boat and swung in himself, revealing long legs in dripping jeans. He sat with his back toward her as he put on his shoes, then reached for the oars as the heavy old boat swung toward her. But she was already floundering away from it, brushing against the mangroves, slipping. She clutched the edge of her canoe with a smothered cry, then lifted a foot to stare in disbelief at the blood running from it.

"Don't you know enough to stay away from those mangroves? There are always big oysters beneath them. Good Lord, that's a hell of a cut."

Lacey looked up. The stranger was staring at her with an expression of pained disgust. She looked back at her foot, at the swirls of blood dripping down into the water, and felt faint. Gripping the canoe with both hands, she rolled in and kneeled, tucking her injured foot behind her, where she couldn't see it. Then she picked up the paddle.

"Where do you think you're going?"

She looked at him in surprise. "Home. Across the bay. My foot—I'll have to do something..."

He swore softly; then, shoving against the bottom with one oar, sent the rowboat against her canoe. His hand shot out and grabbed the line at the bow, which he wrapped around a cleat at the stern of his boat.

"No. That cut is deep. It needs attention now." He settled himself at the oars.

She stared at him, shaken. "I'm quite capable—"she began stiffly, breaking off as the line came tight and the canoe lurched forward. He was rowing, ignoring her. "Listen," she commanded, raising her voice, "I'd rather—"

"Sit back and put your foot up," he ordered, without breaking the rhythm of his rowing. "That will keep your foot from swelling before the cut is washed out."

Lacey felt cold in spite of the warm sun. She leaned back, twisting her legs forward, propping the injured foot on the narrow gunwale, watching the wet blades of his oars rise, dripping and gleaming. The stranger's arms and shoulders gleamed, too, the muscles rolling smoothly. His dark, strong featured face was impassive. She remembered one of the fishermen, relating how he had once stopped at this man's house and had been run off by the combined threat of a shotgun and a vicious Doberman. She glanced at Cabot. At least the cat had claws.

The line of mangroves on the north side of the cove had looked impenetrable, but as they drew near, Lacey saw a hidden cut, a beginning of cleared trail from a small stretch of sandy beach dotted with pebbles and broken shells. The man drove the bow of his boat up on the sand and got out. Wading, he untied the canoe and dragged it in until it grounded firmly. Cabot jumped, a gray blur, landing on dry sand and turning to wait for her. The man's tousled head jerked in surprise.

"A cat? You had a cat in there?"

She sat up, painfully. Her foot had begun to ache. "And you have a dog, I hear. Big and vicious. But still you insisted on bringing me here..."

"The fool dog likes cats," he said, bending to scoop her out of the canoe. He lifted her against his bare chest. "Hold still! And don't let your foot dangle. Hold it out straight."

She had gasped and stiffened as he lifted her; now she strained away from him, pushing futilely, dizzy with pain and fright. "I can walk," she said, her voice high, "Please..."

His arms tightened, and she was abruptly aware of his hard warmth against her breasts beneath the thin knit shirt.

"Stop fighting me," he said impatiently. "You can't walk on these shells, and you're making it damn hard to carry you." His face, inches from her own, stared down at her. "You're scared silly," he added, and his expression lightened. "Why?"

He was so close. She could see the dark shadow of beard on his skin, the faint sheen of perspiration above a firm, broad mouth. His lashes, tipped with gold in the sun, did not hide the waking interest in his sea-blue eyes.

"I am *not* scared. I just don't like being touched." She wondered wildly if that was really true.

"How unfortunate," he said dryly, "since I have to carry you. Just put your arm around my neck, keep your foot out, and the torture will soon be over."

Lacey scowled, but as he started up the trail, she compromised by hanging on to his shoulder. The path, like the beach, was dotted with sharp, broken shells. She watched Cabot stalking ahead of them and was warned by the cat's sudden stop, the rise of stiffening hair on his back. A moment later, a big Doberman bounded into view, and the cat crouched, growling.

"Easy, Max."

The dog stopped, his short tail wagging, and lowered his long head toward the cat. In a moment, Cabot rose and stalked past him, inches from his nose. The dog came on, bumped gently against the man's leg, wheeled, and walked beside him.

"Your cat is smarter than you are," the man said. "He knows when no harm is meant." His gaze slanted down at her; she saw a half-smile and looked away.

"The bleeding has almost stopped," she said, as if she had known it would. She kept her eyes on her foot, on her leg sticking out so rigidly from the crook of his arm.

"If you walk on it the bleeding will start again," he

said, "I'll bandage it and take you home." He paused, frowning. "At least, as far as a dock where you can get help."

There was nothing she could say to that. She clung more tightly to his shoulder as the path turned on a gentle incline. An old house, gray and weather-beaten, stood high in a clearing. Steps led to a sagging porch, a front door with new screening. She tensed as they reached the door and the man swung it open with a finger hooked in the latch. Inside, he eased her down on a leather couch and stood up.

"Won't be a minute," he said, and disappeared through an open arch. She heard his footsteps echoing and guessed he had entered a hall. She looked around the dim room. The couch she lay on was old but comfortable. There was a matching chair, a varnished bookcase full of books, a kerosene lamp above a fireplace. That was it. No rugs, no curtains. She twisted to see the other end of the room. North light from tall windows came in on a tall wooden rack draped with a paint-stained cloth. She heard the stranger coming back and settled into the couch, apprehensive.

He carried a bottle of antiseptic and a roll of bandages in one hand, a steel basin of water and soap in the other; a towel was draped over his arm. Hooking a small stool with one foot, he dragged it to the couch and sat down. He looked huge in the filtered light from the southern windows.

"This will hurt some," he said, and lifted her foot to place the towel beneath it, his hands warm and careful. "Lucky it's not full of mud." He went to work with the soap and water, and she gritted her teeth. "Not too bad, not ragged," he reported, and poured on antiseptic. Lacey squeezed her eyes shut and stifled a sound. When she opened her eyes again, he had moved the basin and was patting her foot dry with a towel.

"Now, a thick pad, strapped tight..." He worked rapidly, his long fingers deft. "Another layer of bandage over that." He sat back. "All right?"

"Great," Lacey said, brushing at her watering eyes. "Lovely. Very soothing." She gave him a sheepish grin.

He laughed, the flat planes of his cheeks breaking into creases, his teeth white in his dark face. "At least you didn't scream," he said, gathering up his supplies. "I'll put these away and take you home. It's getting late."

She sat up. Her foot, warm now and heavily bandaged, felt fine. "You don't have to do that," she said, "My canoe is light and fast, and I can paddle now."

He stood in the doorway, considering it. Plainly, he didn't want to go with her. "Are you sure?"

She stood up and smiled. "See? It's fine, and you've done enough for me. Thank you..." She hesitated. "I don't know your name."

"John."

She looked at him uncertainly. "John what?"

"Doe," he said flatly.

Lacey flushed. "I'm sorry, I didn't mean to pry. I've been a lot of trouble, I know, and I guess I'll still need help getting down to the canoe. But I can manage the rest."

He nodded abruptly. "Be right with you," he said, and went down the hall again.

Waiting, she looked again at the wooden rack and suddenly recognized the T-shaped bottom and draped rectangular top as an artist's easel holding a covered painting. She hobbled to it, curious, and her hand was lifting the cloth before she considered that "John Doe" would have every right to object to what she was doing. After all, peeking would be an invasion of his privacy. She turned away as he entered the room, and was thankful that she had. He glanced suspiciously from her to the painting, frowning. Avoiding his eyes, she hobbled toward the door.

Cabot was just outside, sitting with his yellow eyes fastened curiously on the sleeping Doberman. When Lacey started down the steps, holding the crooked railing, the cat darted ahead of her, ears flat and tail twitching.

"He's angry," the man breathed in her ear, his arms

slipping around her as she reached the bottom step. He lifted her in his arms. "Why?"

"I can walk! I *was* walking..." Indignant, caught by surprise, Lacey struggled but was no match for his strength.

"These shells are sharp, and I don't need another session of bandaging. Relax, will you?"

Silently, she put an arm around his shoulder as he repeated, "Why is your cat angry? Because of Max?"

She shook her head. "The canoe. He hates it, and he gets mad when he knows he has to get in it."

An eyebrow lifted in amazement. "Then why does he get in it?"

"Because I do." She laughed ruefully at his expression. "Please don't look like that. I know it's silly. Cabot is odd, that's all."

"Odd? He's crazy."

She stopped laughing. "Everyone says that, and I don't like it. Cabot is my friend. We live together, and he likes to be with me. I don't see why that's so crazy."

As they neared the beach, they could see the cat sitting in the canoe with his back to them. The man laughed, slanting his gaze down at Lacey. His laughter was strangely seductive, and her stomach made a crazy little flip-flop.

"So you live alone with a cat. Why?"

Her chin firmed. "Practicing. I'm planning to be an old maid."

He stopped on the edge of the beach, still laughing, his eyes traveling over her clinging top and shapely legs. "You'll never make it," he said, and bent his head, closing his lips over hers.

An inner voice told her to push him away, quickly, before... But her mouth was parting below his, and when his tongue touched the tender inside of her lips she made an involuntary sound of pleasure. Of its own volition, her arm slid from his shoulder up around his neck. Suddenly, his grip was tight, his mouth hot, urgent, sliding from her lips to the soft spot beneath her ear, and then, as if he couldn't control it, back to her mouth with bruising intensity. Loud alarms rang in her mind, and she pushed against him, twisting. His arms loosened. Breathing heavily, he stared down at her.

"Don't you know enough not to tease a hungry man?"

She was breathing as hard as he was, her breasts rising and falling beneath the thin shirt, her face flushed. "I'm sorry," she managed. "I didn't mean ... I wasn't thinking..."

With a deep, rough sound he looked away and strode unsteadily across the beach and into shallow water to put her down in the canoe. His eyes cleared as he stood up. "I should apologize, not you. I've wanted to do that ever since I first saw you. It was my fault."

Her lashes veiled her eyes. "Not completely," she said, and picked up her paddle. "I... cooperated." She gave him a small smile. "Call it the response of a grateful patient. And thanks again. I'll replace the bandages and things when I'm on my feet again."

His face changed. "No. I don't want to be rude, but please don't come back. There are reasons—" He stopped, smiling. "Later—in a month or so—will you mind if I come looking for you?"

"I won't mind," she said, surprising herself, and thrust the paddle down to push the canoe into deeper water.

A grin transformed his dark face. "Then tell me who you are and how to find you—please."

The canoe was caught in the ebbing tide, and she raised her voice to answer. "Lacey Thomas. Call me at work. I'm a reporter at *The Clarion*." She was away from the beach now, and raised her paddle in farewell, struck by his sudden silence and the way he stood motionless, staring at her.

Halfway home, she realized that she felt wonderful. Awkward, with the bulky bandage, but wonderful. She paddled strongly, watching the trailing pink clouds of sunset turn gray. Bert and Marie would worry if she didn't get home before dark; perhaps they'd even be out on the dock waiting for her. She thought of the stranger's reluctance to come to this side of the bay. What was he hiding from? Considering logical possibilities, she frowned. He might be a criminal. A drug-runner, perhaps. Florida seemed to be full of them, and a deserted house on a barrier island would be an ideal hideaway. He didn't seem like that kind, but how many of them did?

Cabot leaped to the dock as soon as the canoe nosed in, a soft gray spot blending into the twilight. And then Bert Andrews materialized from the dimness, looking down at them both.

"There you are. Ma and I wondered, but with this weather I figured you were safe enough." He peered at her as she stood up awkwardly. "What happened to your foot?"

"I cut it on an oyster," she said, climbing up on the dock, "but it's fine now."

"Lucky you found someone with bandages," Bert said. "One of the fishermen, I suppose."

She hesitated, looking down at her foot, and then began to walk. "They're always looking out for me, aren't they?" she said evasively. "I'm sorry you and Marie were worried."

Bert was watching Cabot pick his way shoreward over the sagging dock. "Aw, we weren't upset. Figured the boss there would bring you home."

Lacey showered with a plastic bag over her foot, secured at the ankle with a rubber band. She fed the cat and made salad and a sandwich for herself, thinking with regret of the clams, forgotten in the bottom of the canoe. Watching Cabot preen himself contentedly, she remembered how he had sensed the Doberman's friendliness, how sure he had been, walking past those murderous-looking jaws. Instinct seemed to answer a lot of questions.

And cause a few problems. She could not stop thinking of the way that man had made her feel, the way desire had flamed in both of them when they kissed. A sudden, intense desire, frightening in its strength. Even thinking of it now, her body quivered, warmth tingled through her skin. She got up restlessly and limped to the window that looked past the big house and over the dark bay. She couldn't deny that her body had betrayed her today. But John Doe—whoever he was—was exactly what she didn't need. He'd take a woman over so fast she would forget who she was, what she wished to be. A man like that could make a woman into whatever he wanted, and that was something she would not allow.

Chapter 2

"For some, the birds sing..."

The clerk slapped an envelope containing two weeks' extra pay down on Lacey's desk and passed on with an envious sigh. Smiling, Lacey picked up the envelope and stuffed it into her purse. Camping in the Smokies, with two of her New York girl friends whom she hadn't seen for a year, was going to be fun. She went back to writing with renewed vigor. A vacation was just what she needed to get her mind off the man from Fisherman's Cove. Her foot had healed nicely, but her thoughts still strayed to the enigmatic and intriguing "John Doe."

The telephone on her desk buzzed, distracting her. "Miss Thomas? Can you take a call from New York? It's Richard Lonigan..."

Shocked, she wondered how Rick had found her, and then knew. "Put him on," she said, resigned. It was her own fault, inviting Eileen on the camping trip. She should have stuck with just Shelley. Eileen knew Rick, and she loved imparting information.

"Hi, baby! How are things in the hinterlands?" The same bright, amused voice. She could see him—angular, attractive, that lock of hair pointing at one tilted eyebrow, lounging in his chair in the New York newsroom.

"Pleasant, until now."

"After a year, you're still mad? How's Cabot?"

He *would* aim for her soft spot. "He's beautiful. The

best of company." She hesitated, and then, reluctantly polite, added, "How are you?"

"Lonesome. Come back to me."

She ignored that, hearing a note in the brittle voice that told her he was only marking time. "Come to the point, Rick. I know you didn't call to chat."

He laughed. "I can see your smoky eyes looking through me. Actually, I do want a favor. Do you remember Marla Pomeroy? She's about to visit your little town."

Lacey thought back. As an art buff, she had attended many gallery openings in New York, and she recalled having met Martin Pomeroy, who owned the prestigious Pomeroy Gallery. He was a widower, so Marla must be the daughter she'd heard mentioned. "Martin's daughter? I've never met her. Why would she come here?"

"To find Jonathan Grey. You've heard about him. He's Marla's fiancé, and she wants to bring him back up here for the presentation of some award he's won."

"That should be simple enough. If they're engaged, she must know where he is. Anyway, what's *your* interest?"

"That's just it. She doesn't know where Jonathan Grey is. It seems that when he leaves New York he simply disappears for months at a time, and nobody knows where he goes. When he comes back, he brings his paintings for the year. But listen—this is the intriguing part. He's never been seen to lay brush to canvas, and there are an envious few who say he doesn't paint at all—that he pays some unknown to do it for him."

"And you hope that's true, don't you?" Her voice was disgusted. It was Rick's style. He loved to expose the flaws of the famous. In his nationally syndicated gossip column he revealed the awkward intimacies of New York and Hollywood celebrities. Scandalmongering, Lacey called it. If he could prove Jonathan Grey a fake, he would create an international sensation. Grey's paintings were sought by collectors all over the world. Suddenly, a suspicion crossed her mind. No, it couldn't be... "Of course, Lacey, you'll get a fat finder's fee if you can put me on the right track. Marla swears he's somewhere near Tarpon City. I couldn't believe my luck when I found out you were right on the scene. I'll fly down next Monday. I want to see you, anyway." His voice dropped with suggestive warmth on the last words.

"I won't be here. I'm leaving Sunday for vacation."

"You can't! Good Lord, for a story as big as this you can put your trip off, can't you? I'll make it well worth your while—"

Gently, Lacey replaced the telephone, cutting off his frantic voice. She had discovered two things. One, she was completely over Rick Lonigan. Even the sound of his voice repelled her. Two, she was out of her mind. Otherwise, she wouldn't imagine a connection between Jonathan Grey and a solitary drifter who called himself John Doe. She leaned back in her chair and considered the thought of a successful artist, used to every luxury, burying himself in a sagging old house in a swamp. Crazy. Crazier still to imagine that the envious few were right and that "John Doe" was the unknown artist who provided the paintings, while Grey, no doubt, relaxed in some gorgeous condominium and waited until they were finished. She laughed at her ridiculous thoughts, sat up and swung around to face her typewriter again. The telephone rang.

"Our connection was broken," Rick said ironically. "But I thought I'd let you know I'm coming anyway. Be there."

"No. I mean it, Rick. You know what I think of your snooping. But even if I wanted to help you I couldn't. I have other plans."

"You're being stupid, Lacey. Listen, I'll give you credit in the column, build your part up..." He waited, and when she said nothing, he softened his voice. "If you were on to something big and needed help, I'd—"

"Steal my story," she finished for him, and laughed. "Don't you think I know how you operate? Happy hunting—and don't call again. You're wasting money." She hung up, aware of a deep feeling of relief. It had taken time to forget Rick. She had wondered how she would react if he came back into her life; now she knew. But he had puzzled her. It wasn't like him to promise so much for so little help. This story must mean a lot to him. She tried to remember what little she knew about Jonathan Grey. She had never seen him, but she had never missed one of his shows. His paintings were both beautiful and expensive—strange, heart-stopping scenes that ran the gamut from joy to anguish. Some critics considered him a genius. He was one of the few artists to be recognized during his lifetime. Rick had to be off base; Grey couldn't be a fake.

But—his fiancée said he was somewhere near Tarpon City. Abruptly, Lacey got up and went to the managing editor's office.

"Pike, do you know anything about art?"

Pike Farrell was in his seventies. White-haired and frail, he still ran *The Clarion* with an iron hand. "No. Why?"

"Have you ever heard of Jonathan Grey?"

Pike's white eyebrows shot up, and then he smiled, leaning back to prop thin ankles on the desk top. "I keep forgetting you're new here. I guess I could say I know more about art than you know about Tarpon City. I used to know Jonathan Grey, and so did everyone else. He's one of our most embarrassing mistakes. People laughed at him, and when he left, he left for good. He's a native."

Lacey sat down, weak-kneed. "He was born here?"

"Yep. On the wrong side of the tracks, though his grandfather, Frank, was well respected. Frank Grey was a gentleman, but a bit odd. He bought land from a speculator and came down here to find it was in the middle of a mangrove swamp on the other side of the bay. Frank never complained, just built a house on it and lived there like a hermit. I suppose it rotted away after he died. Couldn't get to it except by boat." He hesitated. "But you were asking about Jonathan. Well, his father—Frank's son—was a good-natured bum. His mother was

Kisses Incognito 17

the worker—put Jonathan through school. Then he put himself through an art academy and came back here to paint. Everyone thought it was funny—a brash kid, son of a ne'er-do-well, who thought he was an artist. His folks died young, and Jonathan headed for New York." He smiled faintly. "I guess you know what happened next. Considerable success. Now, suppose you tell me why you're interested in Jonathan Grey."

For once, garrulous old Pike had held her intense interest. Lacey sat staring at him for a minute before she answered. "I might," she said finally, "but not right now."

"Wait a minute." Pike was sniffing news. He sat up. "We could use anything on Grey right now. He just won the International Humanities Award, and we'd sure like a local tie-in..."

"On the women's page?" Lacey baited him. Pike thought female reporters should cover the social news and write cooking columns.

"I'll run you on the front page with a byline," he promised. "Grey has eluded us for years. Do you know him?"

"No comment," she said, and grinned. "I'm sorry, Pike. I haven't any facts—just a hunch. If anything comes of it, I'll let you know." She got up. "After my vacation, that is. Tomorrow's my last day for two weeks."

He groaned. "And you call yourself a reporter. Two weeks! Get the story, if there is one, or someone else will."

Back at her desk, Lacey realized that Pike was right. She should be writing the story now, with the little she knew. She had enough: Grey's fiancée coming to look for him in Tarpon City; the famous Rick Lonigan on the trail of a story right in this little town. She could mention the old house Grey's grandfather had built among the mangroves, and the drifter who stayed there for several months every year. And who *painted*. The story had everything—a celebrity, money, mystery, and love. It would galvanize the entire citizenry and probably be picked up by the national news services.

She could see the results. By Sunday, the traffic on the bay would be terrific—outboards roaring through the cove, with everyone trying to see the mysterious drifter who just might be Jonathan Grey. She stood up, pulled the cover over her typewriter, and went home.

Lacey was packing that evening when Marie Andrews stopped in for a chat. "Boots and a tent," Marie marveled, surveying the litter of camping equipment. "And that thing's a backpack, isn't it? You modern gals amaze me. Three of you, and not one man to scare off the bears. Still leaving Sunday?"

Lacey nodded. "Before dawn, but I'll be quiet. The limousine to the airport goes through town at six, and I don't want to miss it."

"You won't wake us. Now, about the canoe. Bert and I will be away four or five days next week. Do you want him to pull it up in the yard? He's afraid someone will steal it."

"No problem," Lacey said. "I thought of that myself. I'm going to tie it on the car rack and leave it at the garage. They won't mind, and you won't have to worry."

"Good. And while we're gone, I'll have a neighbor feed your cat."

"Cabot?" Lacey laughed, folding the tent. "He's going along. He hates to stay in his carrier while he's traveling, but he loves camping. He'll scare off the bears for us."

Marie giggled. "You and that cat. Who takes a cat on vacation?" She rose from her chair. "We wouldn't have worried about the canoe, but Bert was outside late one night, and he saw a big, rough-looking stranger in an old rowboat near our dock, looking into your canoe. Made Bert think, you know. Middle of the night like that, someone could easily steal it."

"When was that?"

At the door, Marie shrugged. "A week, ten days ago. Bert would have told you, but that was the night you'd cut your foot, and he didn't want to bother you. The man did act suspicious, though. Left in a hurry when he saw Bert coming."

"Thanks for telling me," Lacey said slowly. "I guess I was lucky."

While she finished packing, Lacey argued with herself. It could have been anyone. But Bert Andrews knew all the fishermen. And it was just possible that "John Doe" had been concerned and had made the trip over to make sure she had arrived home safely. He would have had to look closely at the canoe; there were lots of them on this shore, and he didn't know where she lived. The clams, she thought wryly, would have been a good clue. It was oddly pleasant to think he had been worried about her...

In the newsroom on Saturday morning, she hurriedly went through the pink slips from the switchboard operator, glad to note that her replacement could handle most of them on Monday. But the last message made her flush with anger. Mr. Lonigan had called to say that Miss Pomeroy would be in town on Saturday and that he would appreciate any help Miss Thomas could give her. Lacey crumpled the slip and threw it in the wastebasket. Rick never gave up.

It was noon when Marla Pomeroy came into the city room, wearing a white silk suit that spoke quietly but with authority of fashion and money. A tall, slim blonde with an air of confidence, she walked directly to Lacey's desk, looking down with a smile designed to charm anyone into instant friendship.

"You have to be Lacey Thomas," she said. "Rick described you perfectly." She sat down when Lacey greeted her and pulled up a chair. "He tells me you're a crack reporter," Marla went on, "and he's sure you can help me. He did explain the problem, didn't he?"

Lacey nodded, mesmerized by the creamy pallor of Marla's perfectly made-up face, the improbable perfection of her shining blond hair. "He did," she said. "I understand you're looking for your fiancé—"

"I'm looking for Jonathan Grey," Marla interrupted smoothly. "Jon and I haven't announced our plans, and

I wouldn't want them mentioned." She laughed. "You know Rick; he's dying to break the news that we're engaged, but I've told him that if he does I'll deny it. Still, I have to find Jon. This award is important to his career, and the presentation is on the fifteenth, only ten days from now. It's to be made at the gallery, and my father is anxious..." She stopped, searching Lacey's face. "You know this little town. You must have some idea where Jon could be. It's ridiculous, but he simply refuses to let anyone know where he goes when he's in a creative mood. Artists!" Her tone asked Lacey to join her in indulgent amusement. "Always so temperamental, aren't they?"

"I know very few artists." Lacey thought Marla's voice sounded a bit too smooth, too casual. There was an uncertain note underneath all that confidence.

"Why do you think he's in Tarpon City, Miss Pomeroy?"

"Call me Marla, please. My father has mentioned you so often I feel I know you. He appreciated being included in that piece you wrote about independent gallery owners." Marla paused to let the compliment sink in. "As for Jon—I'm sure this is the place he runs away to. He's often told me about the small towns in Florida that are so peaceful and quiet." She laughed. "A town like this is his dream place, if you can imagine that."

"Has he any connections here?" Lacey was almost ashamed of her probing. "Family? Friends?"

"Heavens, no!" Marla sounded as if she thought the question insulting. "He probably picked it for that reason. No one here would know him, so no one would bother him. Frankly"—she leaned forward with a sudden conspiratorial smile—"I wouldn't have known the name of the town myself, but I happened to find an old envelope in his desk. The postmark was the only clue; there was no return address. I was lucky to notice it."

It had become clear that Marla didn't know much about her fiancé. Lacey couldn't resist the next question.

"Where is Mr. Grey from, originally?"

"Jon never speaks of his past. It's as if he didn't have one. His parents are dead, I think, and he's never mentioned a brother or sister." Marla Pomeroy's light voice was beginning to sound bored. "But that has no bearing on the present. Where do you think we should start looking?"

"We? Didn't Rick tell you I was leaving town tomorrow? I won't be able to help in the search. But it shouldn't be hard to find your fiancé in this little town. You must know the kind of place he would seek out." Lacey wondered if she was going too far with her sarcasm, but Marla hadn't listened after the first words.

"You're leaving? Rick was sure you would stay. I'm prepared to pay you very well, and Rick himself will join us on Monday." Her eyes flickered. "You want to see him, don't you?"

"No," Lacey said, "I don't."

"Listen—money is no object to me."

"Nor to me," Lacey said, her temper rising, "and I have no interest in finding Jonathan Grey. You and Rick will make a great team." She stood up, offering her hand. "Nice to have met you, Miss Pomeroy, but I have work to do."

Reluctantly, Marla rose, ignoring Lacey's hand. "Rick will never believe you turned me down," she murmured, with mixed anger and surprise. "He said you'd jump at the chance to dig up a story like this." She swung away impatiently, her heels clicking as she left the room.

And Rick had been right, Lacey thought, slumping back into her chair. Normally, she would have been hot on the trail, glorying in the chance to scoop the New York papers. Guiltily, she remembered Pike Farrell's interest in Jonathan Grey. If Pike heard about this, he would probably fire her, and she wouldn't blame him. Doubtless, Pike *would* hear about it; Rick would be smarter than Marla: He'd head for the editor's office the minute he walked in the door. And when he heard Pike's story about the Greys, the old house...

Lacey drew a deep breath and looked around. She

was alone; the rest of the staff had gone while she finished her work. She leaned forward and dialed a number in New York.

"Eileen, listen. Something's come up here, and I might be late. You and Shelley go on. I'll catch up with you."

Eileen's laughter was knowing. "Rick told me! Wish I had the chance to hunt Jonathan Grey, even with his fiancée along. Well, Shelley and I will keep the same plan. When you get the story filed, you'll know where we are. Happy hunting."

Lacey groaned inwardly. "Thanks. Happy hiking. If I change my mind, I'll be there sooner."

Hanging up, she left the office. There would be just time in the morning if she left early enough and if she wanted to warn the man at Fisherman's Cove, it would be her only chance.

Chapter 3

AS SHE CLIMBED into the canoe and set Cabot down in the bow, Lacey was glad of the Sunday morning quiet, the empty streets. If all went well, the canoe would be back on top of her car, the cat would be in his carrier, and she would be waiting when the limousine arrived. It would only take minutes to explain to the man at Fisherman's Cove that his privacy was likely to be invaded. She was confident that, once warned, he would be resourceful enough to handle the situation.

As the canoe slipped past the yachts with their sleeping inmates and struck out at an angle across the bay, Lacey felt almost exultant. She felt that she was striking a blow for freedom, not only for the man at Fisherman's Cove, but for her own freedom, from Rick and the world of gossip and deceit she had learned to despise.

The night was never as black on water as it was on land. Starshine reflected from the calm surface, silhouetted the uneven outlines of the small islands along the channel. Lacey knew the islands' distinctive shapes, and they pointed the way for her. Even the tide cooperated, pulling her toward the cove. She breathed deeply of the cool air and increased the tempo of her paddling, thankful for her hours of practice during the last months.

The little beach was hard to find. She lost time paddling back and forth along the line of mangroves until a moving form caught her eye. A dark shape, a long, narrow head held high, a stubby tail wagging.

"Max!" She drove the canoe hard, grounding it on the gray patch of sand. Cabot leaped out and Max bounced over to touch Lacey's hand with his damp nose.

"Some guard dog you are," she said irritably. She had counted on him barking an alarm that would bring his master down to investigate. But Max had known her even in the dark. Now she would have to find her way up that trail.

She set off into blackness, bumping into branches, stumbling. She had worn sturdy boots, a denim jacket, and heavy jeans that protected her legs, but she was furious with herself for leaving her flashlight in the car. Cabot had disappeared; Lacey knew he would go straight to the house, but she couldn't see or hear him.

The trail, she remembered, was cut through solid thicket. All she had to do was veer away from heavy branches and keep going. She managed, and when the ground sloped up she grew more confident. There was the square bulk of the house, and she found the steps. At the porch, Cabot brushed against her legs in welcome.

"Thanks a lot for your help," she said pettishly, and the sound of her voice was followed immediately by a thump and footsteps in the house. Evidently, "John Doe" was a light sleeper, she thought, an advantage right now.

She waited, standing near the screen door, aware that she was breathless, even frightened, for she could hear her heart beating in the stillness. Inside, a kerosene lantern flared and she saw her quarry's tousled hair in the light, his strong features blurred by sleep. He set the lantern on the mantel and came toward the door, wearing only a pair of ragged jeans, his bare chest and shoulders enormous in the flickering light.

"Who's there?" His voice was gruff and angry.

"It's only me," she said ungrammatically. "Lacey Thomas."

He flung the door open so that the lantern light fell clearly on her face, illuminating her wide gray eyes and shining black cap of hair. "For godsake, why? What are you doing here in the middle of the night?"

"It's almost morning," she said defensively. She had expected him to be surprised, upset. But his obvious anger shook her. "I came to warn you," she added. "You ought to be grateful. I've been to a lot of trouble. Some people are going to be coming here, searching..."

His arm shot out, and his hand closed over hers, dragging her into the house. "What are you talking about? Who is coming here?"

She jerked her hand from his bruising grasp and rubbed it. "If you'll give me a chance, I'll tell you." She moved away from his threatening bulk. "It's—" She broke off abruptly. Now she could see it. The easel had been behind him, and on it was a finished painting. Even in the yellow light of the lantern she could see that it was a scene of ineffable beauty, glowing colors. A forest, yet not a forest. Trunks of trees flowed into human forms, bending to each other gently in a shimmering grace like faintly heard music. And the forest moved, it seemed, ascending a gentle mountain slope, disappearing into the reaches of a luminous sky. She drew a deep, quivering breath and turned toward him again.

"You are," she said softly, "you really are Jonathan Grey."

With an inarticulate sound of rage, he lunged toward her, grabbed her shoulders, his fingers digging in. "Whom have you told? Who are 'they'—the people coming here?"

"Your fiancée, Marla Pomeroy, and Richard Lonigan, the gossip columnist. And I certainly didn't tell them!" She twisted in his hard grip, pain and sudden anger in her eyes. "Marla knew—"

"You're lying," he said grimly. "They couldn't know, either of them." He let her go, so unexpectedly that she almost fell, and stood staring at her in hopeless fury. "A reporter. And I brought you here myself. I've managed to keep this place a secret for years, and you've broken it wide open. How did you know who I am?"

"I didn't," she said. "Not until now. But I wondered. I've seen your work, lots of it, and that painting doesn't need a signature. Anyone would know it was yours."

She crossed her arms over her breasts and rubbed her shoulders where his fingers had bruised them, staring into his silent, furious face. "Rick Lonigan called me Friday from New York. He said Marla knew you were here somewhere and was coming down to find you—to take you back to receive some award. Then she came to the office yesterday and—"

"You told her where I was," he said bitterly. "Just as you told that columnist. A small-town reporter, and yet you know Richard Lonigan! How much does he pay you for your tips?"

"I used to work with Rick in New York," she said, her chin up, "but I don't give him tips. He called to ask me to help him find you. He's got some crazy idea that there's a secret..." She stopped, looking away. He was furious already. How would he react if she said Rick was trying to prove him a fake? "Anyway, I refused. I don't like the way he works... but he's coming down to help Marla."

"You're lying," he said again, "and I'm tiring of it. No one knows." He turned away, his powerful body like that of a stalking animal ready to spring. The flickering lantern glow made shadows around the tensed muscles along his shoulders. He paced the length of the room and back, coming close, looming over her.

"When will they come? Today?"

She tried to be calm. "I don't think so. They don't know yet about this house—your grandfather's house. But Pike Farrell on *The Clarion* knows; he told me about it." She paused, seeing his hard, suspicious stare. "That was after Rick called. I was curious. Believe me, I haven't told anyone at all! But tomorrow Pike will be in the office—and that's the first place Rick will go."

"To find you, and get all the details." His voice was full of scorn, and suddenly Lacey realized that she might not be able to convince him that she was innocent or that she was only trying to help him.

"Look!" Her voice rose, and she tried to bring it under control. "I'm telling the truth. Rick doesn't even expect to see me. I told him I was leaving today for a two-week vacation, and I am! That's why I came here so early; I'm catching the airport limousine at six o'clock. I left my car at the garage and paddled all the way from the marina just to warn you." She saw his surprised look and pressed her point. "Would I have done all that if I were working with them?"

He stared at her a long moment, and then his broad mouth twisted. "No, you wouldn't. My identity is your discovery, not theirs, and you're making sure it stays that way. Warn me, and I'll leave. They'll hunt, but they won't find me. Then you come back, write the whole story, and play up your part in uncovering it. Very clever."

He wasn't going to believe her. She spread her hands helplessly and then dropped them, turning toward the door. "I give up," she said. "I've warned you, and that's what I came to do. If you want to, you can get away. If not, you'll have the pleasure of seeing your fiancée, anyway. I don't care what you do. And I'll probably miss the limousine—but if I hurry, maybe I can make the next plane."

She was at the door when he grabbed her, whirled her around, and pulled her toward him until his face was inches from her own. "You're going to miss all the planes," he said. "You're not going anywhere, not today or any day, until this is straightened out."

"You can't—" she began furiously, and then stopped. The face over hers held a steel determination. Her eyes widened, and she went pale, twisting, trying to break the grip of his hands. "I won't tell anyone anything," she said, and hated the tremor of fear in her voice.

He seemed not to hear her. His gaze was flickering over her face, her trembling mouth, and the anger in his eyes seemed to fade, to change into something entirely different, more dangerous.

"I've got to get back," she said, almost whispering. "Please..." She twisted quickly, using all her strength against his hands, but he was lifting her, his arms crushing her against his bare chest, his mouth coming down on hers with punishing force, bruising her lips as he forced them apart, taking her by storm. Frantically, she pushed against him.

Her struggles made no difference. Slowly, thoroughly, he searched her mouth, savoring it. When she freed one arm and flailed at him desperately, he seemed oblivious to her blows, ignoring them as one powerful arm slid downward, pressing her closer yet. In panic, she felt his body responding, his passion flaring, and, impossibly, an answering jolt of fire ran through her, burning away her remaining strength. Then he raised his head, low laughter gusting through him as he set her on her feet.

"I'll definitely keep you around, Lacey. I know a place where we can hide from your friends, and no one will find us. You'll provide company—and a certain degree of amusement." He looked down at her with a tight, hard smile. She turned, stumbling, to run.

"Guard, Max." His voice low, casual, he spoke behind her, and on the porch the big dog leaped to attention, tense and still, his eyes gleaming in the yellow light. Lacey grabbed at the door and heard a low rumble of warning as the dog lunged forward, huge white teeth revealed by a snarling lip. She let go of the door, breathing hard, staring at the strong jaws.

"Ordinarily gentle, yes. But trained well. I wouldn't try him, if I were you."

She fought for control as she turned back toward Jonathan Grey. "You can't do this. It's—it's ridiculous, melodramatic. It's kidnapping! Someone will find out..." She paused, hoping to see his expression change, his scornful anger turn to caution. It didn't. "How can you be so—so vengeful? Even if this were really my fault—which it isn't—surely it isn't all that bad..."

He moved then, coming close, crowding her so that she stood between his big body and the tense dog outside the flimsy screen, leaving a space too small for her fear.

Kisses Incognito 29

His face was shadowed by the light behind him, but she saw a muscle bunching along his jaw.

"You don't know what you've done. You've torn up my life. This"—his tight gesture encompassed the room, the house— "this house that seems so barren to you, is the only place where I can be myself. The only place where I can paint—where the old man who loved the child I once was still seems to be present, still encouraging me." He stopped, half-turned from her, rubbing his face with one hand. "You don't know," he repeated, his voice more normal. "This is a game to you. A great splash of a story to sell. Okay. We'll keep it a game, but we'll play it my way." He grinned, the flat planes of his cheeks furrowing. "Relax, Lacey. You're my guest, and some of the game promises to be quite enjoyable." He reached out and ran a long finger down the side of her face, beneath her small jaw, and tipped up her chin. "Fortunately for me," he added, still smiling, "you intrigue me."

She jerked her head away from his hand, her thoughts racing. "You're not thinking," she said tightly, "or you'd know you're heading into trouble. When I'm missed, the search won't be just for you, by two New Yorkers who don't know the bay. It'll be the Marine Patrol, the net fishermen, everyone. They'll find us, and—"

He was laughing in genuine amusement. "Who's going to realize you're missing? You caught the early plane, took off for a two-week vacation, as you unwisely told me yourself. With any luck at all, your famous columnist friend will give up before anyone misses you." He moved to touch her again, but she evaded him, slipping beneath his arm and going to the center of the room, stumbling in her haste.

"Please," she said, "leave me alone." She was sliding rapidly into panic, wondering if she was beaten, fighting against admitting it. Her fear showed, she knew, for she couldn't control her ragged breathing, the pounding of her heart. She made another desperate effort.

"The canoe," she said. "All the fishermen know it's mine. They'll wonder when they see it. Then they'll ask Bert and Marie Andrews, my landlords..."

"They won't see the canoe. I'm not dumb enough to leave it where it is, or my rowboat either. If your friends notice that it's missing, they'll think someone stole it. The old man was suspicious enough when he saw me looking at it once."

So he *was* checking on her that night. He had been concerned enough to make the effort, to ascertain that she was safe. She stared at him wonderingly, searching his face for any compassion, any softening. There was none. She knew that Bert and Marie wouldn't report the canoe as stolen. They thought it was safe in the garage. And the garage manager wouldn't report it, either; he didn't know he was supposed to get it. Jonathan Grey was right. He was safe for two weeks. No. No, he wasn't! She smiled, suddenly triumphant.

"They'll know," she said, almost laughing in her relief. "The garage men will know. I left my car there for servicing, and they'll open the trunk. They'll see my baggage..."

He swore and stepped toward her. Instinctively, she gripped her shoulder bag and swung it behind her, out of his reach. He stopped in midstride and smiled. "You have the other set of keys," he said, and put out an open hand. "I'll take them, if you don't mind. There's just about enough time left to get your stuff before dawn." When she stared at him stubbornly, he cocked his head at her. "Rather we fought for them, Lacey? Would that be more fun?"

Numbly, she handed him the bag, waited, took it silently as he handed it back. The keys dangled from his hand.

"Max knows there's a back door," he said, turning to go. "Don't try it."

She stood where she was, heard his low reminder to the dog as he left, then his rapidly departing footsteps. Slowly, she walked toward the screen door, looking after him. Cabot came toward her in the glow from the lantern, and Max wagged a greeting. But the moment Lacey put her hand on the door knob the dog tensed, growling. Cabot skittered away into darkness. Sighing, Lacey went back and sat down on the couch to wait.

It was well after daybreak before Jonathan returned. The tall windows on the east side of the old house were streaming sunlight over the bare floor. Outside, the deep green of the mangroves glistened as leaves dipped and turned in a gentle breeze. Lacey paced the long room nervously, her mind a welter of discarded ideas, frustrated hopes. At first light, she had turned down the wick in the kerosene lamp and blown out the flame. Sitting in semidarkness inside the screen door, she had watched Max closely. When he lay down on the porch, his long muzzle resting on his paws, his eyes closed, she had gone slowly, carefully, down the long hall to the solid back door. The knob had turned easily, only a faint click sounding as the bolt withdrew, but from outside came the deep rumble of the dog's growl. She went back to the front of the house and watched as Max returned, bounding easily up the front steps to look in at her and then lie down again.

Later, restless, she had gone through the room where a rumpled bed still held the imprint of Jonathan Grey's big body and looked through the window. Max had looked up at her, tail quivering, red tongue lolling from open, sharp-toothed jaws.

"It's a game to you, too, isn't it?" she had asked him, and walked grimly back to the couch. She knew that if she did open the door and step outside, Max might content himself with growling, barking, raising an alarm. He might not leap at her, tear at her with his teeth. Guard dogs were not always taught to attack; she knew that. She considered risking it, and shuddered.

She had begun to wonder if Jonathan Grey had left with no intention of returning when she saw Max rise, stand tensely looking toward the trail, and then relax into a happy wriggle. Jonathan was coming up the path, Lacey's backpack slung carelessly behind him, Cabot's travel carrier dangling from one hand, and a bag of groceries in the other arm. He came up the steps, his unshaven face calm, and paused at the top to nod at the Doberman.

"Okay, Max. Good dog."

She watched bitterly as the dog shook himself, touched his nose to Jonathan's ankle, and trotted down the steps, heading out toward the little beach. Off duty, she thought, since the warden is back. She waited silently, as Jonathan maneuvered himself through the door and set the bag of groceries in the leather chair. Cabot, appearing suddenly, had slipped through the door between his legs and now came to her, raising himself on his back legs, placing his front paws on her knees, mewing. She bent to comfort him, stroking his head.

"He's hungry," she said, accusing. She was, too, a fact she did not mention.

Jonathan laughed. "I doubt it. I found him on the path dining on the remains of a swamp rabbit. He, at least, is resourceful."

She ignored that. "You took long enough," she said. "Weren't you afraid of being seen? Your fiancée gave me the impression she would be going from door to door, looking for you." She was trying to appear as calm as he seemed to be, to act as if they were equals, engaged in conversation. But she shrank back involuntarily as he moved toward her, and was thoroughly embarrassed when she realized he was only handing her the backpack. She dropped it unceremoniously beside the couch, angry at herself for the show of fear. He didn't laugh, though there was a twitch at the corner of his mouth.

"Door to door? A New Yorker? She wouldn't be wandering around the waterfront early in the morning. Probably tucked up in the best hotel she could find, waiting for your friend Lonigan to do the legwork." He yawned. "There was only one car in front of the garage, and the key fit, so I suppose that's your baggage." He eyed the backpack dubiously. "I put it in the boat under a tarp and waited for the harbor supply store to open. My provisions weren't sufficient for company." He gave her an arrogant grin. "I'm sure you can cook. I'm going to take a shower, and I'll want breakfast when I come out."

Speechless, Lacey watched him go into his room and shut the door. She had already found that the bath, furnished with ancient white fixtures, opened from that bedroom. But there was a shower. She had wanted to use it, feeling grimy after plowing up the path, but had been too unsure when Jonathan would come back. Now, she waited until she heard water drumming and then turned and ran out, Cabot at her heels. She flew across the porch and down the steps, making no effort to be quiet.

Max was coming up from the beach. She gasped and stopped short, but he only touched her hand with his nose and turned to follow her. Off duty is off duty, she thought, laughing shakily, and ran on.

The beach was empty. She stood still, her heart plunging. No canoe, no rowboat. Hopelessly, she stared along the green wall of mangroves. The boats were hidden there somewhere, but it would take hours to find them. She had only minutes. She turned to look across the bay at the indistinct line of land on the other side. She could swim, but not that far. And the bay would be dangerous for the strongest of swimmers, because it was bisected by the channel of an inland waterway. As she stood there, one of the many high-powered fishing boats cut through the channel a half-mile away, its propellers throwing a rooster tail of spray far behind it. At that speed, a skipper might or might not see the head of a swimmer in the choppy water. If he didn't, he would wonder momentarily if the object that rolled and thumped beneath his hull had bent one of his expensive propellers. She turned and walked slowly back up the path, Cabot preceding her, Max walking sedately by her side.

Jonathan emerged from the bedroom, toweling his hair, as she came in. He was dressed as usual, except that his cutoff jeans were not ragged. He grinned at her.

"Very good," he said. "A walk before breakfast improves one's health, especially after a confinement. Fresh air, all that. But I'm still hungry. You'll find bacon and eggs in that bag."

"No, I won't. I don't intend to look for them." She went stiffly to the couch and sat down.

The towel still in his hands, he came to sit down beside her, his broad mouth still smiling, his sea-blue eyes unreadable. "Odd. I would have sworn you were the domestic type. Are you sure you don't want to cook?"

"I'm sure." She resisted the impulse to leap from the couch, to run from him again. That hadn't worked. Maybe if she made herself as unpleasant as possible, he'd be glad to let her go.

Sighing, he laid the towel aside. "Too bad. But I'm not unreasonable. Perhaps I'll cook for both of us. First, though, I'll show you what I'm really hungry for."

He was too big to move that fast. She was pinned by his arms, pressed down into the yielding couch by his weight, her nostrils filled by the scent of soap, of a musky shaving lotion. Her protesting cry was muffled by his mouth on hers. Then his hand was beneath her jacket, pulling up the tail of her shirt, sliding beneath it. She caught his thick wrist, circling it with her hand, thrusting it away with all her strength, and still the hand moved upward effortlessly and closed gently around her breast. Flame shot through her, and then outrage. She arched up with her whole body, fighting his weight, her fear drowning in a flood of anger. He raised his head and looked at her with mock surprise. She burst into tears of rage, turning her face away, feeling his hold loosen. Slowly, his weight lifted from her, his hand slid gradually, caressingly, from her breast.

"There's no pleasing you," he said. "I suppose now you'll say you'd rather cook." Plainly, he had enjoyed his revenge.

She lay still, breathing deeply, until her heart stopped its heavy pounding. Then she pulled herself up and stood, taking off the denim jacket, tucking in her shirt. Her eyes were smoky, furious, as she moved to the chair and picked up the bag of groceries.

"I'll cook," she said. "It certainly beats the alternative." She stood watching the dark flush that spread over his face and then went toward the hall, heading toward the kitchen with quick, decisive steps. She knew she had touched his pride with her scorn, and was bitterly triumphant.

She had seen the kitchen when she explored the house. A stove and refrigerator, both of which ran on propane, both comparatively new. A cabinet that held plates and cups, a neat sink, a wide counter. She unloaded the bag and found the bacon and eggs and also a carton of orange juice, coffee, fresh bread. And a dozen cans of cat food. She hadn't expected him to think of Cabot. It was even stranger that he would bring enough to feed the cat for days while providing only breakfast for himself and for her. She stacked the cans thoughtfully. Evidently, there would be food for humans where they were going, but not for cats. She began stripping bacon into a cast-iron skillet.

They ate, silently, at a trestle picnic table on the porch, with Max in eager attendance. Thoughtfully, Lacey held a piece of bacon toward the long jaws. Max looked at it hungrily and turned his head away, saliva dripping.

Smiling, Jonathan took the bacon and held it out. Eyes shining, Max gulped it, and Jonathan looked at Lacey amused.

"He accepts food only from me. Which prevents poisoning—of either body or loyalty."

Lacey flushed. It had been the dog's loyalty she was after, and she didn't deny it. "You can't blame me for trying," she said, and looked him in the eye. "I don't give up easily."

He laughed, sounding as if he meant it. "Fair warning," he said, "and thanks for a good breakfast." He stood up. "When you finish the dishes, unload the food from the refrigerator and cabinet. Put it all in the barrel inside the back door. But keep the cat food in your backpack. Turn off the gas; the valve is on the wall behind the stove."

"Where are we going?" She hadn't expected to leave in daylight. She had thought they would wait until dark, when she might have a chance to escape.

He grinned, and she wondered if he had read her thoughts. "To my hideout, to enjoy your vacation." His grin softened as he studied her, and his hand moved to touch her hair. "Black silk," he said, sliding his fingers through it, "soft and shining... Too bad it covers such a deceitful little head."

She had tensed at his touch. Now she sat still as his hand dropped away, alert to the change in his voice. He had sounded—well, not scornful. Maybe... She stood up briskly, reaching for the dishes.

"Cleaning the kitchen makes sense," she said. "I gather you want the house to appear deserted."

"Exactly. But don't try to do it all. We'll have help. I made a couple of telephone calls this morning while I waited for the harbor store to open." He grinned at her and whistled for Max, who came running. "I'll put Max on guard again. It works both ways, you know. He won't let anyone in, either, until I come back."

She had stepped inside and now stood with the dishes in her hands, staring at him through the screen. "Who would try? No one comes here."

"Who knows?" He sounded bitter again. "Yesterday, I thought that was true, but you seem to have changed the pattern." He turned his broad back on her, gave the dog a command, and went down the steps.

"Where are you going?" He had moved so quickly she had to call out to stop him. He looked back, his eyes glinting.

"Don't tell me you'll miss me, Lacey. I know it's only professional curiosity. I won't be far and I won't be long. I have to meet someone."

She leaned against the door, watching, thinking how changeable he seemed. Earlier, when he had spoken of his fiancée, he had sounded more sarcastic than affectionate. Almost as if Marla Pomeroy's expected intrusion were that of an irritating stranger. Marla would have to exert all that polished charm when— Her elbow, bent with the weight of the dishes, touched the latch of the screen door. Outside, Max raised his hackles and growled ominously.

She jumped. "Oh, you—" she said, exasperated, and headed for the kitchen again.

Chapter 4

LACEY COULD HEAR the deep throbbing of engines only because the morning breeze had abated, leaving the air hot and still. It was after she had finished in the kitchen, taken a shower, and put on clean shorts and a shirt. She was stripping the sheets from the bed, but as the sound grew closer she left the work and went to the window, pushing damp hair from her forehead, leaning on the sill to listen.

It had to be a large boat in the cove. The sound was too heavy and close for anything else. Someone searching, so soon? The engines muttered and were still. She strained to listen, in a quiet so profound that she could hear Max panting below the window. Why had the boat stopped? She had a sudden vision of Marla climbing down into a yacht's dinghy, being rowed along the shore by some man, searching for a way in.

Below her, Max sprang to his feet, looking toward the path. Lacey moved back from the window nervously as three men rounded the curve of path, talking together, and laughing. The one in the middle was Jonathan. Lacey stepped forward again, and he left the others and came to stand below her.

"Sorry," he said, amused. "These are my friends, Charlie and Rolf."

Lacey sighed. "I was afraid it was Marla Pomeroy."

"Afraid? I would think you'd welcome her."

"Not her," Lacey said firmly, "though I'd be delighted

to see the Marine Patrol." She turned her back on him and busied herself in folding the sheets, collecting towels, soap, and shaving cream from the bath, packing them all into a cardboard carton. The room was taking on a deserted look, an air of being abandoned, unused.

In the big room, the men were busy; she had kept track of them furtively. They had packed Jonathan's books and hidden them in a tiny attic. From a large closet they had dragged out canvases, tied them in muslin bags, and slid them carefully into a large, slotted case. Between their moving bodies, Lacey could see the paintings only as snatches of color and form. Jonathan, leaving them, went all through the house, checking it over. She noticed how quickly they moved, how efficiently they worked, as if they had done this many times before.

She sat down in the big chair, feeling invisible. Neither of Jonathan's friends had looked at her or spoken, though the younger of the two seemed awkwardly aware of her when they passed. She studied them, seeing the dark, sunburned look of seamen, yet wondering at their clothes. Beside Jonathan in his cutoff jeans, they were ridiculously well dressed in smart white mid-length shorts, lightweight white shirts, open at the neck, expensive deck shoes. The older one—a broad-shouldered, heavy man of perhaps fifty—was quiet and dignified, with an air of command. The other—young, tall, and slender, his light hair bleached almost white by the sun—seemed less sure of himself. Any thought she had of appealing to them, trying to enlist their help, was lost as she watched them with Jonathan. They not only seemed to know him well; they actually deferred to him.

"Everything of yours in that backpack?"

She jumped. Jonathan was looking down at her from behind the chair. "Yes, everything. And the cat food."

He nodded absently, his eyes traveling over her tan hiking shorts, crisp, long-sleeved shirt, heavy socks, and sturdy shoes.

"Nice for mountain climbing," he said. "That's all. I'll have to do something about your clothes."

"Simple," she said. "Send me to the mountains."

He laughed, his brows arching up in surprise, and then went to hold the door open as the other two men struggled out with the case of muslin-wrapped paintings. Then he picked up the nearest box and followed. She went to watch them going down the trail, and Cabot, looking harried, came to the screen door and mewed.

"Don't worry," Lacey told her pet. "I'm not going anywhere without you." She went back and sat down again. The cat was the only thing left of her normal world. It seemed impossible that only yesterday she had been sitting in the *Clarion* office planning a camping trip. She had belonged to herself, had been able to make her own decisions. One of them, she thought wryly, had landed her here, turned her into a prisoner. She set her jaw. There would be an opportunity to get away, sooner or later. She would be ready to take it when it came.

A half-hour later there was nothing left to suggest recent occupancy of the old house. Furniture covers, wrinkled and gray with dust, had been brought from a tiny attic and thrown over the couch, bed, and chairs. The men, coming and going, had left a sifting of sand, scattered dead leaves on the bare floor. They had carried the barrel of discarded food and packages out the back door and disposed of it in the swamp. The windows were closed and locked, and in the heat the musty odor of old wood had already permeated the air. Standing in the middle of the big room and looking at the draped furniture, the bare and gloomy walls, Lacey was sure that any stranger would think the house deserted long ago.

Jonathan had come back alone to make a final check of cabinets and closets. Now he took her arm.

"It's time," he said. "I hope it's not too late." He hurried her outside, his hand tightening as they went rapidly down the steps. "Marla called the police, told them I was here somewhere, and asked them to find me."

"How do you know that?" Even her uncertainty, her resentment, couldn't keep her curiosity down.

"Friends," he said briefly, leaving her to wonder if

he meant the two men who were here, or if someone else was involved. She was silent, thinking how strangely serious he was about this place, how much trouble he was willing to go through to keep others from knowing he used it. Even his fiancée. Of course, if this plan worked, he could come back and paint in privacy again, and no one would know. Except her. Would he trust her, eventually? Believe her when she said she would keep his secret? She speculated on what he might do if he didn't trust her, and her fear of him came back full force.

As they rounded the curve, the beach lay ahead, and she saw that a small boat was drawn up on the sand. In the middle of the cove was the source of the engine noise she had heard: a yacht that dwarfed the cove with its size, close to fifty feet of sleek power. The stern of the boat was toward the beach, the name clearly visible in large black letters: *The Hideout*. Lacey gasped and looked up at Jonathan, finding his glance amused.

"You'll find the yacht a bit more comfortable than the house," he said.

The younger man, Rolf, was still winching the dinghy into place on its stern davits when the engines started with a spitting roar and Cabot shot away from the stern, his hair on end, to find refuge on the forward deck. Still grasping Lacey's arm, Jonathan took her into an enclosed lounge where a blast of cool air from a humming air conditioner met them.

"Sorry, but we'll both have to stay out of sight until we're in the ocean. Yachts are common enough in the waterway; no one will recognize this one. If you're out of sight, I may be in the clear." He grinned at her as they moved out of the cove into the channel. "We're due for a celebration." He crossed to a small bar. "I ordered all the amenities, so I'm sure there's a bottle or two of wine in here, chilling. Make yourself comfortable, Lacey. Sit down."

At a loss, she took the nearest chair. Bentwood and cane, with white vinyl cushions, it matched the rest of the furniture. A table topped with Plexiglas, a chaise longue covered with a nest of yellow pillows. A small couch bracketed with end tables, three more chairs, gimbaled lamps, and thick, soft blue carpet under her feet.

She accepted a brimming glass of white wine from Jonathan, trying to appear composed. She sipped, looking up at him through long lashes. "You've gathered together a lot of luxury in here," she remarked.

"I bought this boat from a tired old man who had had an extravagant young wife. Wait till you see the cabins." He sat down in the nearest chair, his broad, bare chest and worn jeans looking as out of place as she felt.

"You said something about the ocean," she began carefully. "Will you tell me now where we're going?"

"Cruising." He slanted his eyes at her, sipping his wine, and then laughed. "You may as well know. We're going to the Bahamas. I expect a certain amount of gratitude. It's a better vacation than you had planned."

"It is not."

"You'd rather tramp around in the mountains than play on glorious beaches?" He was relaxed, and clearly enjoyed teasing her. Then, abruptly, he sat up, staring through the wide windows of the lounge. The engines had slowed, the yacht's bow dipped, and then it slogged slowly ahead. Jonathan let out his breath and leaned back into his chair again.

"Manners," he said, and laughed. "Charlie's a good skipper. Meticulous about courtesy on the water. He slowed down to cut his wake for a fisherman pulling nets near the channel."

Lacey leaped from her chair. Her hand was pulling at the sliding door when he caught her and dragged her away from it, twisted her around to face him.

"I'm going to have to be more careful, I can see that," he said. "I forgot you know all the fishermen, and you nearly made it, didn't you? One good, loud scream and the party would have been over."

"I wasn't going to scream," she said defiantly. "I was going right on over the side. He would have picked me up." She was furious with herself for not having thought of it, for not being close enough to the door.

In the wheelhouse, the unseen Charlie gunned the engines sharply; the yacht's bow thrust up into speed again, and the motion tilted Lacey into Jonathan's arms. He steadied her, leaned down, and kissed her lightly before she could draw away. "Don't fight so hard," he said softly. "You can't win. I'm doing something I have to do—to keep my life the way I want it. It won't last long. If it goes well, you'll be free again by the time your two weeks are up." His sea-blue eyes were almost sympathetic as he looked down at her. "Can't you bear with me?"

She gazed up at him, wishing she had the courage to ask him what would happen if things didn't go well, and where he got the nerve to ask her to bear with him—in other words, to cooperate in her own kidnapping! But the look on his bronzed face was almost pleading, and the firm mouth that had kissed her so gently had left a sweet taste of wine, of tenderness. Angry at her own indecision, she pulled away from his warm, bare flesh and went back to her chair.

"I can't promise you anything," she said. "I haven't any reason to trust you."

After a moment, he nodded and came back to sit beside her. "Nor do I have any reason to trust you," he said. "I don't know why I asked. Guess it was just a silly hope that the trip could be pleasant, since it has to be made." His face was again set, unreadable.

An hour and a half later, they left the channel of the waterway and headed east through a small inlet to the ocean. The yacht's engines began a subdued roar, bucking an incoming tide. Looking through the windows, Lacey saw the familiar yellow flag flying from a boat coming toward them, the flag flown to alert everyone that the boat was returning from foreign soil and on its way to check in at Customs. Her heart leaped as she turned to Jonathan, trying not to appear eager.

"We'll be checking out at Customs, won't we?"

He gave her a wry look. "Looking for another chance to get away, aren't you? Charlie did all that this morning on his way up. We're legal—destination, passengers, everything." He stood up, stretching, and went to the sliding glass door. The yacht had begun a gentle rise and fall as it neared the mouth of the inlet, and as he opened the door, warm, salty air blew in, the breath of the ocean. After a moment, he shut the door and returned to his chair.

"Nice. A two- or three-foot sea, that's all." He picked up a magazine, adding, "Another fifteen minutes and you'll be free to move around."

She looked away from him, tense and silent.

Once in the ocean, the yacht moved easily over the slopes of the sea. Restless, Lacey rose and went to the circular section of windows at the stern. Beyond the foaming wake, the distance to the receding shore looked endless, and the water was now the deeper blue of open sea. Sprawled in comfort on the afterdeck, Max lay asleep in the sunshine, and Cabot sat beside him, staring out to sea with flat, disgusted ears.

"It can't be helped." Jonathan had moved as quietly as any cat; his voice was close behind her. She turned, startled, and looked up into the blue depths of his eyes. Then she spoke in a rush of words.

"When this is over—when they've given up searching for you—are you going to trust *me?*" She was unaware of the fear in her wide gray eyes, the quiver of her lips.

His face softened, and he reached for her, clasping her shoulders in strong arms. "That depends on you, Lacey." When she tried to twist away, he held her, and then cupped a hand on each side of her face, tipping it up. "So beautiful, so stubborn," he said softly. "Do you remember the first time I kissed you? I can't seem to forget it..."

She jerked away, remembering how she had returned that kiss, how shamelessly she had clung to him that first day.

"That was before you called me a liar, before you made a prisoner of me," she said furiously. "I didn't know you then." Her voice was high and angry, lashing at him.

His smile faded. "Didn't you? When you peeked under the cloth on my easel, didn't you at least suspect? I didn't know then that you'd recognize my work, but I know now. Isn't that why you called your friend—or maybe more than friend—Richard Lonigan?"

She wanted to hit him. Her hands ached with it; she could almost feel the satisfaction of a hard slap on his scornful face. She clasped her hands together tightly to prevent herself from acting on the impulse. "I didn't do either of those things. I didn't call Rick. I admit I wanted to look at the painting—and I almost did. But at the last minute I didn't. It—it seemed like prying."

He muttered an incoherent oath and swung away from her, his body tense, as if he, too, had been holding back violence. "Forget it," he said over his shoulder. "I've tried to believe you. But there isn't any other way they could have known. I wish—" He stopped, swallowing the rest of what he was about to say. Then he added, "You've got the freedom of the boat, now. Go anywhere you want. If you go through that door beside the bar, you'll find the cabins. The first one is mine. Yours is at the end of the passage."

He was gone, through the sliding door onto the deck. She watched him pass the windows, striding forward, tousled hair wind-whipped above a grim face.

The passage, reached by going down a three-step companionway, was paneled in teak, lighted by a series of portholes along one side. There was a door set in the opposite bulkhead, and another door faced her at the end. The cabins are too close together, she thought, too isolated from the rest of the boat. When she reached the end of the passage, she was relieved to find a key hanging in the lock. She took it and pushed the door open. Stepping inside, she found herself fighting a hysterical impulse to burst into laughter. The old man who sold the yacht to Jonathan must have had a very extravagant young wife. Lace frothed over the bed like a sea of white waves, falling in tiers to deep blue, thick carpeting. Enticing mermaids sported across the headboard of the bed, while dolphins leaped, soaring, on the posts. Someone had brought her backpack in; it lay on the bed looking positively embarrassed. She walked in, and from the mirrored wall behind the bed her reflection walked toward her—a slim, black-haired young woman in hiking shorts, tailored shirt, and heavy shoes. A highly unsuitable outfit, she thought, and then she did laugh, turning away from the mirrored wall, wondering in spite of herself who had occupied this cabin on Jonathan's other cruises. Whoever she—or maybe there had been a succession of shes—had been, Lacey was willing to bet the woman or women hadn't worn hiking clothes in this cabin. Much more likely a glamorous negligee.

She touched the smooth top of a dressing table beneath a porthole, opened a door, and found a small but elegantly appointed bath. Thick towels, the same blue as the rug, hung by the shower.

The cabin also contained a small storage chest and a wide but shallow closet with louvered doors that folded out of the way. A small chair, a bedside table. Luxury and comfort, she thought, and realized that here, in the middle of the large boat, the sound of the engines was muffled, the motion of the sea hardly noticeable. She sighed, thinking how delighted she would be if she were a guest, off on a Bahamian vacation, instead of a prisoner—an unwilling hostage...

Taking shorts, shirts, and her lingerie from the backpack, Lacey left the heavy clothes in it and put it away. If she had a chance to escape, she could grab the backpack and go. While she put her things away, she thought of what Jonathan had said about not fighting so hard. Perhaps if she acted as if she were trying to make the best of it, he would be off guard. Most of the islands, she knew, had airports. If she could get away, she could be back on the mainland in an hour. And he hadn't confiscated her purse; she had more than enough money for a ticket. Worth a try, she thought, and then smiled. It shouldn't be too hard to pretend to enjoy this.

She put on fresh lipstick and brushed her hair, feeling a rising sense of excitement and anticipation. Then she took off her heavy shoes and socks, wriggling her toes gratefully in the thick carpet. She had no deck shoes, but she could go barefoot. She went back to the lounge and, feeling privileged, slid open the door and stepped out.

The yacht that had seemed so huge in the cove was small in an infinity of blue. Leaning against the rail, Lacey was arrested by the surrounding beauty—the deepening blue of the eastern sky as the world rolled toward night, the pink and orange flowering of sunset in the west. Her hair blowing in the fresh breeze, she watched a school of flying fish rise in sparkling scatter from the edge of the bow wave, glide through the air a dozen yards before diving below the surface again. Then she felt a soft touch on one ankle and looked down at Cabot, who stared up at her with anxiety in his yellow eyes. She dropped to sit cross-legged on the dock, gathering him into her arms.

"A rude surprise, isn't it? All water, no land." She stroked him, tweaked an ear, and laughed as he batted her hand away. "No problem, Cabot. We'll go home soon, and we have a sumptuous cabin." She got up, still holding the cat, and turned to see Jonathan lounging against the bulkhead behind her. He was wearing the crew uniform—shorts, open-necked shirt, and deck shoes. He had shaved, and his bronze skin gleamed in the glow from the sunset.

"Sumptuous? Does that mean you approve?"

She tried a bright smile. "It's lovely." She shifted the cat's weight, looking down, her lashes veiling her eyes. "I'll admit the next week or so may not be so—so bad, after all." Her gaze swept up, finding his expression quizzically amused, and she rushed on. "The ocean seems so close—so different. You can see so much more..."

That pleased him. He relaxed visibly. "In the Bahamas," he said, "you'll see more. The water there is gin-clear—like looking through glass." He gave her a sudden, hopeful smile. "You could hardly help enjoying it."

Lacey laughed, feeling triumphant. It might be easy to make him think she was having too much fun to leave. "Sounds wonderful," she said. "But right now I think I'll put Cabot down in the cabin. He's had enough of wind and water."

Jonathan followed her into the lounge. "Don't be long," he said as she started down the passage. "We're having an early dinner. Rolf is outdoing himself, with company aboard."

"Great," she said. "I'm starved..." She caught his puzzled stare as she entered her cabin and cautioned herself. It wouldn't work if she overdid it. She put Cabot down and went to wash her hands, wondering at the pleasurable tension she felt. The man was too magnetic... and she was too susceptible. She went back out and found Cabot sprawled on the little chair, looking boneless and sleepy. I could take lessons from him, she thought, in how to look relaxed and self-possessed.

In the main saloon, the steering station was deserted. In this weather, Charlie was on the flying bridge overhead. Lacey looked curiously at the shining galley and dining area, sniffed the tantalizing odors that reminded her she hadn't eaten since breakfast. Rolf, his silver-blond head bent over the salad he was tossing, looked up and smiled at her shyly. She smiled back, conscious of Jonathan's glance as she seated herself on an upholstered bench at the table.

"Something smells delicious," she said to Rolf. "What is it?"

"Scampi," he said, looking past her at Jonathan. "I hope that's all right."

There was an odd inflection in his voice, Lacey thought. As if he didn't refer to the dinner, but to something else. Was he trying to find out if it was all right to speak to

Kisses Incognito 49

her? She looked at Jonathan quickly and found him still watching her—and his blue eyes were doubtful.

"It's certainly all right with me," she said, determinedly cheerful. "I love scampi." Relaxing into the soft cushions, she gazed around with what she hoped was an expression of admiration. "Beautiful," she added, glancing at Jonathan. It was, too. The sun had sunk below the low clouds, and the saloon was lighted by gimbaled brass wall lamps that glowed on the teak walls and gleaming chrome of the galley, added color to the deep gold of the upholstered benches. She gave Jonathan a slow smile meant to dissolve his doubt, and saw his expression change to sudden amusement.

"Nice to see you so contented," he said, and sat down opposite her as Rolf brought salad and wineglasses to their places. Jonathan's eyes gleamed as he reached into a cooler beside the table, brought out a bottle of wine, and poured. "Isn't it a rather quick change of mood?"

"I suppose so," she said carelessly, "but why not? When you can't win, it's foolish to fight." She was proud of how nonchalant she sounded, how steady her hand was as she picked up her wineglass. "Anyway, who could help enjoying this?" She looked at him over the rim of her glass as she sipped, a mere flicker of a glance that accepted his amusement and added her own.

He laughed, raising his glass to her in silent salute. "I'm with you," he said, and added softly, "a pleasant place to be."

She felt flushed with success as she pitched into the plate of sizzling scampi Rolf placed in front of her. The aroma of butter and wine, the faint whiff of garlic that rose from the plump, broiled shrimp, made her ravenous. The crisp salad and delicate wine were perfect accompaniments to the scampi, and she ate steadily, almost ashamed of her hunger when she looked up and caught Jonathan's surprised gaze.

"Sorry," she said, laughing, "I simply couldn't stop..."

"It's the sea air," he said gravely, "a great stimulant

to the appetite." He looked at her empty plate. "Would you like more?"

"I would," she said, "but I haven't room."

"A tribute to my cooking," said Rolf, coming to place a bowl of fresh fruit and a small platter of cheeses between them. He smiled down at Lacey, his glance showing unmistakable interest, and she was cheered by the sudden hope that he would be her ally.

"I rank you among the great chefs," she said, and smiled into Rolf's eyes with as much charm as she could muster. "My compliments."

He grinned, his young face flushing with pleasure, but across the table Jonathan spoke abruptly.

"The great chef is probably hungry himself," he said, "and also Charlie. I'll take the wheel while they eat, and I want you with me." He rose, and Lacey, recognizing an order, rose with him. She followed him meekly up the steps that led to the flying bridge.

Charlie, greeting Jonathan with a relieved grin and Lacey with a mumbled "Good evening," disappeared rapidly down the steps into the saloon, closing the hatch behind him.

The canvas canopy that sometimes covered the flying bridge had been lowered. The open sky was winking with stars, pale still in the first darkness. From this height, the ocean looked calm; only the rise and fall beneath her feet told Lacey the small waves were still there. There were two seats, but she stood, leaning against the frame of the windshield that wrapped around the bridge. She looked out over the darkening sea, watching the lights and indistinct shape of a ship in the distance.

"When will we reach the islands?"

"Some time tomorrow," Jonathan told her.

Surprised, she left the windshield and sat beside him. "Really? I've always heard it was a short run—only hours in a fast boat like this one." She was leaning toward him, studying his face in the dim light, wondering why he suddenly seemed so cool and reserved.

"It is. But we'll spend tonight and part of tomorrow anchored behind the Lily banks. There's someone I want to see." He fell silent, his face still and impassive. She leaned back, waiting.

When the silence had lasted long enough, Lacey stirred and sat up. "I think I'll go to my cabin," she said. "Cabot must be very hungry."

"Rolf fed him fresh fish," Jonathan said, and put a hand on her arm. "He even made a litter box for Cabot, back on the stern. You'll find Rolf very thoughtful." His fingers closed on her arm, tight and warm, but she couldn't see his expression now. "You will undoubtedly like Rolf very much as you know him better. But he, like Max, is loyal. It may save you some embarrassment if you remember that."

She pulled her arm away and stood up, glad of the darkness that hid her face. "It must be very nice to have friends you can count on," she said, trying to keep her voice even. Was there anything she could think of that he wouldn't guess? Was she that transparent?

"You can count on me. You won't be hurt, Lacey."

"I hope not," she said, her voice quivering, "but it's hard for me to trust someone who doesn't trust me." She left him quickly, nodding to Charlie and Rolf in the saloon, going down the steps to the deck and on to the lounge, where she paused just long enough to pick up a magazine before going on to her cabin. Once inside, she closed and locked the door, thankful for the key. Cabot was sound asleep on the chair, and she didn't blame him. It was hard to believe that everything that had happened since she left her apartment had occurred in only a day. She thought of how she had taken the cat out of his carrier and started off in the canoe, planning to be back in time to catch that limousine...

After undressing, she searched through the clothes she had unpacked, but found nothing to wear to bed except heavy, too-warm pajamas, packed for the cold nights in the mountains. Impossible, even with the air conditioning. Shrugging, she turned back the lacy coverlet and climbed into the ornate bed, ignoring the sportive mermaids on the headboard. She pulled a sheet up over her naked body, grateful for the silken smoothness, the softness. The magazine held her interest for only a few minutes, and when her eyes began to droop she turned out the lamp and snuggled down sleepily into the rumpled bed.

Chapter 5

SOME TIME DURING THE night the engines had stopped rumbling. Lacey remembered that as she opened her eyes in the morning, though she couldn't have said when it happened, only that the sudden quiet had wakened her for a moment. And now there was silence and hardly any movement. The yacht seemed as steady as dry land. She turned her head and saw clear blue sky through the porthole. It was late. She had slept well past her normal waking hour and was still dazed and drowsy. And cold. Cold? She realized it was the drift of a wavering current from the air conditioner on her bare skin and sat up, startled, to pull up the sheet that had twisted down below her waist. Then she remembered that she couldn't be seen from the porthole, that the cabin door was locked. She tossed the sheet back to scramble from the bed and head for the tiny bathroom, yawning hugely.

She showered, searched out her only short-sleeved blouse, her lightest pair of slacks. Standing, she could see blue water through the porthole, calm as a farm pond, glazed over by sunlight. It must be very late, she thought. She was hungry, and Cabot would want to go out on deck. It was odd that he hadn't wakened her, jumped on the bed and mewed, as he did when she overslept at home. He wasn't on the chair. She knelt to look under the bed.

"Come out, Cabot," she said crossly, "wherever you are."

In minutes, she had satisfied herself that the cat wasn't in the cabin. Nor was the door locked, for it swung open at a touch. Her face flaming with anger, she marched through the passage into the empty lounge and out onto the deck, where she found Cabot sitting contentedly, his yellow eyes half-closed against the glare of sun on water.

"You traitor," she hissed, "who let you out?"

Behind her, she heard the scrabble of padded feet on the deck, and Max's nose bumped her in enthusiastic greeting. She turned, seeing Jonathan coming toward her from the forward deck, wide awake, alert, and with an infuriating smile on his face. She drew herself up.

"I locked my cabin door," she said icily, "because I wanted privacy. Does that mean nothing to you?"

His smile deepened. "Not much, when a cat is mewing desperately on the other side of the door. Besides, you looked lovely—and cool. Perhaps too cool? When I find a place to shop, I'll buy some appropriate clothes for you, including a nightgown." His eyes were warmly intimate, teasing, and her face flamed again.

"That won't be necessary," she said. "I'll make do with what I have." A picture of herself half-naked in that frilly, seductive bed had sprung clearly to her mind, and embarrassment nearly choked her.

"I'm afraid you can't make do. In the places we'll be visiting, you'll have to be dressed as if you belong on the boat. Hiking clothes would attract undue attention, don't you think? Someone might wonder about you and ask questions." He was still smiling, but his slanted gaze was suspicious. "Or were you counting on that? Don't let your pride bother you. I'll consider the clothes a business expense, not a gift." He gave her a conciliatory glance and took her hand. "Don't be angry. The cat really wanted out. It seemed a shame to keep him cooped up in there just because you were sleeping late."

"He would have wakened me," Lacey began, and then remembered she was supposed to be friendly. "It's all right," she said lamely. "It was nice of you to consider him." She could barely get the words out, watching Jonathan hide a smile.

"No need to thank me," he said. "It was a real pleasure." He turned, still holding her hand. "Come and have breakfast," he added. "Rolf is getting anxious."

Lacey went with him up the companionway to the saloon, let him seat her at the table. Rolf, busy in the galley, greeted her warmly and poured orange juice and coffee, gave her a choice of sausage or ham with her eggs.

"Just toast, please," Lacey said, smiling. Rolf's tanned face was fresh and healthy, and his hazel eyes met hers with a look that was more than friendly. She sipped her coffee slowly, toyed with the buttered toast until Jonathan excused himself and left. Then she looked at Rolf invitingly.

"We're anchored on the Lily banks, aren't we? Have you been here before?"

"Often," he said, coming eagerly to sit with her, "but we're not on the banks; we're inside them. The water near the banks is shallow. They protect this spot, keep it calm. It makes a nice place to wait."

"Lovely," Lacey agreed, looking out at the sheen of blue water. "Whom are we waiting for?" She tried to ask the question carelessly, as if she had thrown it in simply to make conversation. But she could see that Rolf was immediately on guard.

"Just a friend of Jon's," he said, and got up hurriedly, offering her more coffee, clearing the table when she refused. He busied himself in the galley, washing up, polishing the chrome, efficient and silent.

Lacey watched him, reflecting bitterly that Jonathan had been right again. There would be no help from that quarter. Or from any other quarter. If she managed to get away, she would have to do so by her own efforts. She had never felt so alone, so helpless. She pushed her toast aside and got up, managing a smile as she thanked Rolf and left the saloon.

The deck was deserted, except for Cabot, who now sat near the rail, looking down at the water with his ears pricked forward, his body tense. Wondering, she went to stand beside him and became motionless with surprise. She was looking down into a giant aquarium. A suitably artistic composition of coral and sea fans rose up out of patches of sand and seaweed. She watched a heavy grouper move from beneath an overhanging coral shelf, ponderous and slow, its threatening presence sending small, brightly colored fish darting away from it. Sea anemones fluttered their flowerlike tentacles, urchins waved their sharp spikes, and the growth of green and tan weeds in the white sand bent and flowed back and forth gracefully in small, invisible currents. A ballet, she thought, and surely that crab, perching on a coral head and waving its pincers, was directing an unheard orchestra.

"Better than television?"

She jumped, and then laughed halfheartedly. "I'll never get used to your silent approach," she said. "You're a born footpad."

Jonathan leaned on the rail beside her. "There's an advantage in surprise. Watch that 'cuda if you need proof."

A long silver and black barracuda lay motionless in a shadow. In the clear water, Lacey could see every scale, the faint flutter of small fins beneath the creature's gills, the glitter of wicked-looking eyes. It's resting, she thought, bored by the calm scene. There was nothing important nearby, only a sparkling, darting mass as a school of tiny minnows played, drifting past. She jumped at the explosion of swirling sand and water as the barracuda shot forward, jaws chopping, body twisting, as it snapped up the fleeing minnows. In seconds, the predator was lying in the shadow again, as immobile as before.

She looked at Jonathan soberly. "I thought the barracuda was ignoring those minnows," she said, "too bored to bother with something so small."

"A mistake commonly made," Jonathan said, "and not only at sea." He stared south, his eyes narrowing, and added, "Our company arrives—a good hour early." He glanced at Lacey. "You will stay in the lounge."

She didn't like taking orders, but in the last day and a half she had learned that it was useless, and sometimes unwise, to argue with him. She went obediently toward the lounge, then lingered at the door to watch the approaching boat. It was fast. Even faster than *The Hideout,* she thought, noticing the man in the bow. Slim, tanned— hair almost as light as Rolf's. And naked except for a wisp of French bathing trunks. Then she saw his binoculars and slipped quickly through the door, glancing back at Jonathan. He was frowning, displeased.

In minutes, the other boat slowed and bumped softly against the rope fenders hanging on the side of *The Hideout*. The blond man leaped to the deck beside Jonathan, clasping his hand, thumping his shoulder, grinning. Lacey watched, standing behind a drapery, thinking she had never seen a man so devastatingly handsome, so elegantly made. He could have been modeled by a sculptor. All slender grace, perfect features. Slender enough, in fact, to make Jonathan look like a bear beside him. A not too pleasant bear, frowning, his jaw set. Then Jonathan turned and strode toward the saloon, the slim stranger keeping pace with him, expressive hands moving as he talked.

Lacey shrugged as they disappeared, then sat down and picked up a book. Whatever the reason for this secret meeting, it had nothing to do with her. Once it was over, they would go on to the populated islands, where there were airports. Until then, she could only wait.

A quarter-hour later, hearing noise on the deck, she went again to the window. This time, she stood well back, for the stranger was facing her and she saw his dark eyes flick over the glass. But then the scene grew too interesting for caution. Charlie and Rolf were carrying the case of paintings to the rail, straining with the weight of it. On the other boat, two crewmen waited, looking expectant.

A transfer at sea. Did this constitute smuggling? She

knew Jonathan's paintings were valuable, but she was completely ignorant of Customs law. Perhaps works of art were exempt. But if they were, why such elaborate secrecy? She watched the crewmen carefully lower the heavy case into the other boat and take it swiftly below. Then her gaze returned to the stranger and a still-frowning Jonathan. The stranger was no longer laughing, but serious. Were they arguing? Then Jonathan shrugged and nodded, and the two of them left the rail, coming toward the lounge. Lacey dashed for her chair and book.

"Lacey?"

She swiveled in her chair and looked up with what she hoped was an expression of surprised welcome. Jonathan was entering the lounge, closely followed by the other man.

"This is my friend Lance Randall," Jonathan said, and Lacey noted that his smile did not reach his eyes. "He has relieved me of my—problem. The rest of our vacation will be carefree, darling." He leaned down, hiding her from the stranger's view. Tipping up her chin, he dropped a light kiss on her mouth before she could pull away. Astounded, she gazed up at him and saw the warning in his eyes before he turned away.

"Lacey wants nothing more than to leave this godforsaken spot and head for Freeport and Nassau," he said, his voice humorous and indulgent. "Nature bores her. I think she's a bit frivolous."

She would have to go along with him. She had little reason to trust Jonathan, but even less to trust Lance Randall, who might be a smuggler, and whose brown eyes were searching her face suspiciously. She smiled at him and leaned back in her chair, stretching and then curling up seductively. "Frivolous? I'm as serious as I can be—about having a little fun..." She let her gaze rove over Lance's handsome face. "You can understand that, can't you, Lance? You look—very understanding." She managed to inject the phrase with flirtatious admiration, and saw his face relax into a smile. His brown eyes now ran over her with practiced skill, a look that assessed her slim curves as if her clothing were transparent.

"Absolutely," he said, "and if this idiot doesn't see to it that you enjoy yourself, call on me." The tension had left his slim body, the smile he turned on Jonathan was ingratiating. "Glad to see you're relaxing," he said, clapping Jonathan on the shoulder. "I'll be off, and I'll see to that errand..." At the door, he turned back and looked at Lacey. "See you, honey. Treat him right. He's needed someone like you for a long time." Jonathan moved between them, but not before she saw Lance's meaningful grin and wink.

She sat staring at the door after they left, knowing precisely what Lance Randall thought she was doing on the boat, and realizing that Jonathan had set it up to look like that. She felt vaguely insulted, even though she had played along. When Lance's boat pulled away, she stood up and looked after it, watching the wings of spray appear as it picked up speed and rapidly became only a white dot on the horizon. Outside, she could see Jonathan standing on the deck watching also, his face stiff and still. Then he opened the door and came in.

"Thank you," he said. "You did that very well. Almost too well. But it wouldn't have been necessary if you hadn't stayed on deck long enough for him to see you through his binoculars. He insisted on getting a closer look, unfortunately." In spite of the words, his voice was critical.

"I'm sorry," she said. "Sorrier than you might think." She eyed him coldly. "I certainly don't like being taken for one of your—one of your..." She stopped, unable to think of a word to describe what she meant.

"My what?" His face was no longer quite so stern, and his eyes glinted.

"Your methods of relaxation," she snapped. "Like the other...*ladies* who have slept in that sexy boudoir you call a cabin."

He looked completely surprised, and then his deep laughter filled the room. When she turned away from him, even angrier, he came and took her shoulders, forced her around to face him.

"Are you trying to tell me you didn't enjoy giving that sultry treatment to Lance? The little smile, the starry eyes, all that beautiful body language? I can't believe it. You had me convinced, too." He was still laughing, and she gave him a look of resentment.

"I was only following your lead," Lacey said.

Jonathan held her gaze, his eyes darkening. "Keep following," he said, his voice dropping seductively as he pulled her close. "Maybe it's time for one of those enjoyable interludes I promised myself." His arms went around her swiftly, his mouth came down on hers, but this time his kiss was gentle, warm, and seeking, and a traitorous impulse welled up inside her, making her want to respond...to press even closer, to yield completely... The angry warning in the back of her mind could not drown out the wild beating of her heart.

"Lacey..." His voice was a breath of sound, muffled against her lips. "You were made for this." One strong hand was tangled gently in her hair, the other stroked slowly down her back to bring her closer yet against him, and at once the flame of her own desire leaped high, strong enough to frighten her. She put her hands against the wall of his chest and pushed, twisting her mouth away from his.

"No!" A strangled whisper. "No! Stop..."

"Why?" The circle of his arms was too strong to break, but his voice was soft. "Don't spoil this, angel. You want me, I know you do."

"Let me go." She kept her face averted, refusing to meet his eyes.

"Look at me." His hand came up and turned her face to his. "Look at me and tell me you don't want me."

"I can't," she said, her mouth trembling. "I have n— normal feelings. But..."

"But what?"

"But it's wrong!" Her own weakness had made her angry, and she lashed out at him. "You—you're taking

Kisses Incognito 61

me—like something you own! I'm your prisoner—and you're counting on my fear of you to make me give in."

He let her go so suddenly that she stumbled away from him. The warmth had left his face in an instant, and he looked coldly furious.

"Are you truly frightened of me, Lacey?"

"Of course I am! You've got me out here in the middle of nowhere, and everybody is on your side. My friends don't even know where I am; they don't know I'm in trouble. And how do I know what you might do? You—you won't believe me. You think I'm a danger to you..." Her voice was beginning to break, and she stopped and breathed deeply, her chest heaving, determined she would not cry or plead. "You think I'm just a woman," she added, "but I'm *me.*" She was past the point of worrying about how silly that might sound; she was merely proud of having gotten the words out in a voice that no longer broke or trembled.

"You seem to know a lot about what I think," he said, his voice distant. "Are you sure you're right?"

"Yes! You proved it this morning. You don't regard me as anything but your property—or you wouldn't have unlocked my door like some Peeping Tom, looked at me when I—when I didn't know it." She felt again the angry embarrassment, knew her face was coloring, and was angrier yet when he gave a short laugh.

"You know why I opened that door, Lacey. As much for you as for your cat. I knew you were tired out and needed sleep. I thought I'd let Cabot out before he wakened you. When I looked in, I didn't expect to see anything except a huddle of bedclothes." His set mouth softened, twitched as he looked down at her contorted face. "Do you always sleep naked?"

The question infuriated her. "Never again on this boat," she snapped. "I've learned that."

"You haven't learned a thing," he said, and came close to her again, looking at her as if she were a truculent child. "Do you know how you looked, how inviting? The Song of Solomon couldn't do justice to the beauty of your breasts or the curve of your waist..." His hand came up again and turned her face so that she had to look at him. "Your arms were flung open, waiting for an embrace. The hardest thing I've ever done was shut that door and walk away. But I did it. I didn't have to, you know. I'm master of this boat. I could have taken you, as you put it, right then." He stared into her wide gray eyes a moment longer and then dropped his hand and turned away. "Forget it," he said. "It won't happen again. Now, if we're to make Freeport today and Nassau tomorrow, I'd better get Charlie started."

She watched him through the window as he left, thinking how calm he was, how much in control of everything around him. Even when he was wrong, he managed to twist things around until he sounded right. It was getting to the point where she had to remind herself that he had kidnapped her. She set her jaw and left the lounge, wandering aft to look for Cabot.

At the stern, Rolf was raising a blue canvas awning to create a welcome patch of shade against the sun, now high and bearing down with tropical intensity. Max and Cabot were already taking advantage of it as Rolf fastened the last grommets. He looked up and saw her as he finished, and came to meet her with eager admiration plain on his face. "Sandwiches and iced tea in the saloon, Miss Thomas. We'll be under way soon."

"Call me Lacey, please." She spoke before she thought, out of a need for friendliness, but when a look of pleasure swept his face she was glad she had.

"Thanks, I will," he said, smiling. "It's a pretty name."

She smiled and followed him toward the saloon, hearing the anchor chain clank up on the bow and then the sudden, thrusting roar of the diesel exhausts. Perhaps Rolf might yet prove an ally; it was a faint hope, but she had no other.

Chapter 6

LEANING ON THE rail beside her, Rolf gestured at the narrow tip of the large island called Grand Bahama. "West End," he said in a tone only slightly bored. "We never stop here."

Lacey gazed longingly at the stone jetties that offered safe harbor, the big hotel outlined against an impossibly blue sky. "Why not?"

"Jon doesn't like it," Rolf said. "There's nothing here but the big gambling casino and the International Bazaar. A money place. Exciting, but not typically Bahamian." He paused, and then added, "We're going on around the island to Freeport."

Lacey felt a stir of hope. "We'll stop there?"

"Only to refuel and pick up supplies," Rolf said, "Then on to Nassau."

Lacey's hope changed to an alert excitement. To refuel, they had to go to a dock. If she had Cabot in his carrier and her wallet in her pocket, she might be able to get off the boat quietly while Jonathan was busy. Once off, she would break and run if necessary, counting on bystanders to intervene if Jonathan tried to bring her back. If I have to, she thought, I'll scream. She was suddenly tense, her hands curling tightly on the rail. It was a chance...

"We're having lobster thermidor tonight," Rolf said, and Lacey jumped at the sound of his voice, startled out of her thoughts. "What's the matter? Don't you like lobster?"

"I love it," she said weakly. "I guess I was—just dreaming."

"Dream of lobster," he said, laughing, "and leave those nightmares alone. I make a very good thermidor." He left, striding along the deck toward the saloon, and Lacey wondered what he would think if she said a hamburger at a Florida drive-in would suit her better, at least tonight.

Freeport was easy to recognize. Ships clogged the sea lane; jet aircraft swooped overhead. The horizon was jagged with huge hotels and condos, and the waterway teemed with every kind of vessel that would float. Lacey's excitement grew. She had taken Cabot below and locked him in his carrier, picked up her wallet and stuck it in the pocket of her shorts. She was burning with eagerness as the engines slowed and *The Hideout* turned. She could see fuel tanks ahead, towering over the flat landscape. Glancing forward, she saw Jonathan settling into the pilot's seat. She went quickly to the door of her cabin.

Carrying Cabot, she kept well away from the paw stretched out through the holes in the carrier, claws bared as the cat growled. "It's for your own good," she whispered, setting the carrier just inside the door of the lounge. "We'll be back on land, soon, I promise."

At the window, watching, she began to grow uncertain. The docks they were approaching looked too big to be real, even from a distance. They grew taller and taller as the space between them and the boat grew smaller, and when *The Hideout* finally came to rest, her heart sank. The dock surface had disappeared above her line of sight. Only the huge pilings beside the boat attested to the fact that there was a dock somewhere up there. She stepped out on deck and looked up, staring at the bottom of the planks she had hoped to step out on, realizing at last that these docks were built for huge ships.

Up on the higher level of the bow, Jonathan was tossing a coiled rope to a dockhand above him, while Charlie was reaching for the dangling nozzle of a fuel hose being passed down by another man. She looked back again at the edge of the planks over her head, measuring the distance, wondering if she would be able to stand on the rail and pull herself up. Then she looked back again at Jonathan and saw that even though he was on the bow, his hands didn't reach the dock.

She stood there, sick with disappointment. The heat was terrific, the sun beating down through still air, reflecting from the oily water, full of debris, that swirled around them. Beneath her feet, the deck seemed scorching. Then Jonathan came from the bow, smiling.

"Watch that first step," he said. "It's a big one."

She hated the ridicule in his voice, hated even more knowing that he had guessed her plan and had known it was impossible. But she pushed down the angry retort that rose in her throat and managed a wry smile.

"I had heard Freeport was a place to gamble," she said. "I was willing to try."

His brows rose, and he laughed in surprised appreciation. "It wouldn't have worked, anyway," he said. "I'm not willing to let you go." He had stopped beside her, his gaze amused but still questioning. She felt again the electric jolt that came whenever their eyes met, and she looked away.

"When will you be willing?"

"That depends on several things," he said obliquely, "including you. I know it's boring to be confined to the boat, and maybe eventually we can do something about that. I might feel I could give you the freedom of the island once we get to Nassau."

Her heart leaped. Didn't he know that to her the freedom of the island meant the airport, and total freedom?

"That would be nice," she said, not looking at him. "I might like to do some sight-seeing, or something."

"Of course," he said agreeably, "but in the meantime, the lounge is air conditioned and a lot cooler than this deck. If your gambling fever has subsided, you might be more comfortable in there." He grinned as he added, "And your cat might appreciate his freedom, too."

She gave him a smoky glance from under her lashes

and left, going to the lounge, where she knelt beside the travel carrier and unlocked the door. Cabot stalked out and sat down, giving her a glance every bit as baleful as the one she had given Jonathan.

"You'll be free again before long," she said to him softly. "And then I'll be free, too." She got up and went to sit in her usual chair. She blamed herself for what she saw now was childish stupidity. Jonathan knew exactly what he was doing, where he was going. If there had been a possibility that she could have escaped, he would have been more careful—maybe confined her to her cabin—she knew he had a key!—or set Max on guard again. Escaping was not going to be easy, she could see. But there had to be a way, she thought stubbornly, somehow, somewhere...

Refueling seemed to take a long time, but finally the lines were cast off; the boat turned from the dock and headed out into the busy channel. Lacey settled herself for another long run. Then she realized they had turned north, and her head came up alertly. Nassau lay to the south; she knew that. She watched the shoreline, the gaily colored sails of the small catamarans as they careened past, and realized they were again moving out of the channel, nearer to the island, going slowly, picking their way. Then the engines cut off abruptly, and she heard the anchor chain rattle. A moment later, the creaking of the davits that held the dinghy brought her out on the deck in time to see Jonathan, dressed like a member of a ship's crew, climbing down into the small boat with Rolf. She went to the rail and watched as they started the small outboard and chugged toward shore. Then she went forward to find Charlie.

"Supplies," Charlie said in answer to her questioning. "And some other things Jonathan intends to buy. They shouldn't be too long." His heavy body lounged in the pilot's seat as if he had rooted there, as if the flying bridge were his natural home. Lacey stood below him, her feet on the middle step of the ladder, only her head and shoulders above the opening of the hatch, and looked

Kisses Incognito 67

at him carefully. He looked solid and sensible. His brown hair was graying along the sides; his eyes in their deep pouches of wrinkled brown skin looked calm and kind.

"Charlie," she said impulsively, "is there any way I could persuade you to—to help me get off this boat?"

"No." His voice was regretful, but no more so than if she had asked him for some ordinary favor that he was unable to supply.

"Kidnapping is a serious crime," she said, "and you could be named as an accessory. But I suppose you know that." As far as she could see, her words hadn't caused him to change his expression.

He sighed. "From what I've heard, you got yourself in trouble, Miss Thomas. I guess you'll have to get yourself out." He gave her a sudden grin that folded a hundred wrinkles into his sun-dried skin. "I don't think it will be as hard as you believe. Don't worry about it."

There was a tone of finality in his voice. She went back down into the saloon and then out on deck, where the sun-warmed surface burned her bare feet, forcing her to retreat hurriedly toward the lounge. This time, when she sat down, Cabot jumped into her lap and settled there, purring.

"I thought you'd gone over to the enemy," she said, stroking him. It was true. Not only had he actively resented the carrier more than ever, but every time she had gone looking for him he had been with Jonathan's big dog. After only twenty-four hours on the yacht, he had stopped flattening his ears. He seemed contented. Cats, she thought, didn't waste a lot of time butting their heads against stone walls. She leaned back in the comfortable chair and put her feet up, relaxing.

Later, she heard Charlie walking back and forth on the deck outside and then the sound of a sputtering engine. Sitting up, she looked out. Charlie was dropping the long, rope-covered fenders over the side and she could see a patched and gaudy canvas canopy bobbing toward the yacht. She jumped up, dislodging the cat, and went to the window. The canopy belonged to a small, open launch now easing itself up to the side of the bigger boat; a black man in ragged cutoffs and a T-shirt was standing in the bow with a line to toss to Charlie. She stepped out and, feeling the blistering heat of the deck beneath her, thrust her feet hurriedly into the cool shadow of the rail as she looked down.

Two women stood in the cockpit of the smaller boat, surrounded by boxes. Two amazing women, one a smooth-skinned Asian and the other a tall and elegant black, both casually draped in brilliantly colored cloth that left their shoulders bare. Both were wearing wide, ingratiating smiles as they looked up at her. Lacey looked at Charlie, who was coming aft again, this time with a ladder to hook over the side.

"Who are they?"

"Women from the bazaar, I would say," Charlie told her, and put the ladder down to them, securing it at the top.

The women scrambled up as if this were part of a daily routine and turned to accept the boxes and bags that the black man held up to them. Laden, the Asian woman turned to Lacey with a bow of her shining head.

"I am Madame Li, and this is Ada, my assistant. We have brought everything that was ordered," she said. "What we did not have we found in other shops. All you need to do is see if the clothes fit. Though now that I see you I am sure the sizes are right. Perhaps a hem or two to alter, but we have brought a sewing box."

"I ordered nothing," Lacey said, staring at the beautiful face, the exotic, almond-shaped eyes, the charming smile. The woman's shoulders, rising above the draped cloth, were as smooth as porcelain. The cloth was brilliant scarlet, with a border of golden seashells painted on it. Her laugh, trilling forth, was indulgent.

"The captain ordered them, miss. All these, bought and paid for. Please, show us where to put them. You must try them on."

Lacey looked from her to the black woman, who smiled at her over the pile of boxes she held in her long, graceful arms. Lacey could think of nothing to say, and turned to Charlie helplessly.

"Do as they say, Miss Thomas. If the clothes are paid for, believe me, they'll never make the return trip."

Return trip. Lacey gave him a startled, quick smile and turned back to the two friendly women, who now looked less like saleswomen and more like rescuers. They might not take the clothes back, but perhaps, a paying passenger... She led them through the lounge and down the passage to her cabin, hearing their murmurs of admiration for the luxuries. In minutes, clothes overflowed the bed, the chest, the small chair. White and pastel; shorts, thin, low-cut cotton blouses; high-waisted, pleated slacks in cool fabrics. Two handfuls of satiny black material that resolved themselves into a bikini; a silver-lilac one-piece suit that wasn't much more substantial. Nightgowns, silky and seductive. A modest, two-piece shirtwaist dress in light coral silk. Sandals, deck shoes, pumps. Stockings, and, tumbling out of one box, three lengths of bright, soft cotton in turquoise, flame, and light green, bordered with silk-screened flowers and shells.

"Pareos," Madame Li said, smiling, "like ours. You can wear them so many ways..." She waved a hand at the black woman. "Ada will show you."

Taking an unmistakable model's stance, Ada smiled and her hands moved swiftly, untying knots. Her pareo swirled free, exposing a taut body clad only in brief panties, then floated down again as she retied the fabric in an entirely different style. Again, and this time she wrapped the top, dipped down, and brought one end of the cloth between her legs and up around her waist to tie it into a bloused and fluttering body suit. "I'll leave it so," she said, smiling at Lacey. "Best for climbing down ladders, don't you think?"

"Inventive," Lacey said, laughing, wondering how long it would be before she could broach the subject of leaving with them. "Everything is beautiful," she added, and started putting the clothes helter-skelter into their boxes. "Of course, I'll keep them."

"But they must be fitted." The Asian woman reached out quickly to take a coral skirt from Lacey's hands. "See? This is much too long. Here, try it on. You will need it in Nassau. You will wish to visit places there where you cannot wear shorts or slacks."

That was something she hadn't considered. If she couldn't escape to the island with these women when they returned, she would have to make her break in Nassau. There it would be easier to melt into a crowd, to remain unnoticed, if she wore suitable clothes. Quickly, she began taking off her shirt and slacks.

They kept her busy, insisting that she try everything on, pointing out that it was their duty to see that each garment fitted correctly. The captain, they said, must feel he had got his money's worth. They even had her drape and tie a pareo. "From Martinique," Madame Li said proudly, "from St. Anne's. See, each one is signed by the designer." Her gaze was speculative as she watched Lacey knot the material over her high, thrusting breasts. "Now," she said, "the bathing suit."

"It will be fine," Lacey said, impatient. "There is no way to alter it, in any event."

"But if it doesn't become you," the woman said softly, "Mr. Grey will not be pleased."

Lacey sighed and put the one-piece suit on, looking at herself in the mirrored wall. "Too much," she said, "or rather, too little." The silver-lilac was a taut second skin, molding her body into deeper curves, accenting her breasts, exposing a flare of her hips almost to the waist with its sharply cut sides.

Madame Li smiled. "But it will please the men, will it not? And that must be the prime consideration." Her eyes were friendly but cynical, her meaning unmistakable. Lacey flushed, silently removing the suit and putting her own clothes back on. First Randall and now this woman had taken it for granted that she was in the business of pleasing wealthy men. She swallowed her sharp retort; there was no reason to make the woman angry when she wanted a favor from her. She watched the women make the small alterations, and when they had finished she waited until Ada had picked up the boxes and tissue paper and carried them out. Then she faced Madame Li squarely. She would have to be frank, because Charlie might try to stop them.

"If you will take me to the island on your boat," she said rapidly, "I will pay you well. But we will have to be quick and quiet. The crew member aboard will try to stop us."

The woman's lashes flickered down over her almond eyes. "The captain said you might ask, since you were disappointed not to be allowed to visit Freeport." She spread a small hand in a gesture that said men were so unreasonable. "But I'm afraid he also said I was not to bring you in. He intends to leave soon and does not want to wait."

Lacey stared at her. It was apparent that the woman knew something was not quite right, and it was just as apparent that she intended to have nothing to do with it. "But I have been *kidnapped!* I'm being held against my will. Does that mean nothing to you?"

"It means you have a lively imagination, miss. Criminals do not buy finery such as mine for their victims. If I were to take you away in my boat, *I* might be the one accused of kidnapping."

Lacey's lips trembled. "Then—will you pass on a message for me? A call to the States? I'll pay you."

The woman cocked her head, considering. "Why not? That would be no trouble for me."

Hurriedly, Lacey searched her purse for a pen and a memo pad. She wrote down Pike Farrell's name, the telephone number of *The Clarion,* and a brief message, her fingers shaking. Pike was to call the Bahamian police, report that she was being held on an American yacht, *The Hideout,* and must be taken off. She gave the next port of call as Nassau and signed it simply Lacey. She knew how bizarre and incredible it sounded. She didn't care. She knew Pike would do it, if only to find out what idiocy was afoot. She handed the message to the woman, went back into her purse, and brought out a hundred-dollar bill.

"Call during business hours," she said, "and be sure to talk to Mr. Farrell. Tell him exactly what I have put down, no more. Don't mention that you have talked to Mr. Grey, or that Mr. Grey owns this boat." Somehow, she thought, she would try to protect Jonathan, to keep the old house on Fisherman's Cove a secret. That seemed important.

The woman took the note and the money, her small hand closing over it eagerly. "It will be easy to leave Mr. Grey out of it," she said, "for I do not know him. Only his captain and his boat. Everyone knows *The Hideout*." She smiled. "Of course, the name of Grey is familiar. There is a great interest in art at the Bazaar."

Lacey was puzzled. "His captain? Young, slim, very blond?"

The woman's eyebrows rose. "Indeed not. Large, dark-haired, and broad-shouldered. In his thirties, I would say. Have I been taken in?"

An irresistible impulse overcame Lacey. Perhaps she could get rid of the unwanted clothes, after all. She raised her brows as quizzically as the other woman had. "I sincerely hope not," she said. "Did he pay by check?"

The puzzled look disappeared, followed by a light laugh. "No. I may be mistaken as to the man's identity, but only my pride would be hurt. He paid in cash." Moving quickly, she gathered up the remaining clutter. "Bon voyage, my dear. I believe I have understood correctly; you do not wish to give me your full name. No matter. When you wish to try modeling, come to me. In the meantime, of course, I will give your message to Mr. Farrell." She hurried through the passage, and Lacey heard the noisy engine of the launch begin to splutter again.

So Jonathan hid his identity even here, in the islands. That must be why he wore the crew uniform. It was an efficient disguise. Aboard *The Hideout* he could use the name and influence of Jonathan Grey and still remain anonymous. It was a great plan for a man who wanted no publicity. Anyone who wished could find out who owned the yacht; documented vessels were easily traced. Yet they would think only the crew was aboard.

Putting the clothes away, she thought of the complex character of the man who held her prisoner. He truly did value privacy—at least, his own—more than anyone she had ever met. A loner, maybe. Yet he made solid friendships, if the loyalty of Charlie and Rolf was an example. And he was thoughtful and discerning in some ways. She had to admit that everything he had bought for her—with the possible exception of that daring bathing suit—was something she would have bought for herself if she could have afforded it. Naturally, an artist could pick the best colors for anyone, but he had even chosen the right sizes. She considered that, and then took the turquoise pareo from the drawer where she had put it. With the thin gold chain she always carried as a necklace, it would be cool and attractive for late afternoon and evening. It wouldn't hurt to show Jonathan her appreciation. It might even help to soothe his feelings later, when a representative of the Bahamian government boarded the boat and escorted her ashore. Lacey began to laugh softly to herself, wondering how she could manage things so that Jonathan wouldn't be arrested as a criminal.

An hour later, showered and dressed in the pareo, she had worked out her plan. She wouldn't press charges, of course. How she would explain later to Pike she had no idea. But she was sure she could convince the Bahamians that there had been no crime of any kind. She would simply show them her press credentials and tell them she was writing a series of articles about the islands, and had wanted to know how quickly they would respond to a crime involving a visitor. They might be very angry, or, on the other hand, they might be pleased by the idea of good publicity for their tourism. But no matter what they thought, she would be free.

Chapter 7

AT FIRST LIGHT they were idling slowly along the island of New Providence, entering the harbor of Nassau. Jonathan had sent Charlie below to have breakfast. He had brought Lacey to the flying bridge with him, and together they were watching the outlines of the island grow clearer through an early morning mist. Lacey, dressed in brief white velour shorts and a soft, scoop-neck pink blouse, leaned on the frame of the dew-damp windshield, not bothering to hide her excitement. She was full of new confidence, aware that if the dressmaker had succeeded in talking to Pike the afternoon before there might even now be policemen patrolling the docks, waiting for *The Hideout* to appear. If not, if Pike had left for the day when the call came, she would get him this morning. It could only be a matter of hours...

Lacey had made the previous evening as pleasant as she could. For once, she hadn't begun an argument. And Jonathan, though somewhat cool and reserved, had responded by treating her with exquisite courtesy. The dinner had been excellent, and afterward they had sat in the lounge in silence, listening to the stereo as they cruised on a calm sea toward Nassau. Evidently, Jonathan had been trying to show her a bit more respect, for he had made no further attempt at intimacy, had indeed bade her good night rather early and gone to his cabin. It would have been perfect, she thought, if only he had been less moody.

"Look!" Her hand flew out, pointing. A magnificent cruise ship had materialized from the mist, lying at a huge wharf. The masts of sailing boats near jutting quays were becoming clearer; Lacey could see their drooping sails, the graceful curves of their hulls.

"The colors," she breathed. "Everything is so bright."

"No brighter than your eyes," Jonathan said dryly. "So little time at sea, and you're dreaming of dry land. I hope you can wait."

"I can wait," she said, "as long as I know I'll make it." She had turned her face away, afraid of her own look of triumph; now she glanced back and saw him studying her, his gaze traveling up from the snug velour over her hips, resting on the curve of her breasts at the low neckline of her blouse, then, surprisingly cold and unreadable, reaching her eyes.

"Nice to have you happy," he said, "but you'd better go below. I'll be docking this monster in a few minutes, and you might prove distracting." When she looked at him in surprise, he added a clear warning. "I'm sure you know you're not to leap to the dock and run. I put Max on guard before we came up."

Troubled, Lacey went below. Walking aft to the lounge she began to worry. Max in snarling defense of the boat would make the authorities more than suspicious. They might not believe her when she explained that Jonathan was innocent. She looked for Max as she went, and saw him sitting near the rail, alert and tense. His eyes followed her intently as she entered the lounge.

She sat on the edge of her chair as they passed the wharf and then the quays, where she could see natives unloading the distinctive Bahamian sloops, carrying baskets heaped high with fruit. The reaches of the city were becoming clearer through the mist, the masses of trees, the hotels, the big warehouses that lay behind them, an ancient fort. The whole place seemed both tropical and English, a strange mixture of pink and white island houses and stately government buildings. She could have enjoyed this, she thought, if it weren't for this feeling of imminent disaster. What if Jonathan refused to let the police board the boat? That, and Max, would convince them there had been a crime. The whole story would come out.

I don't care, she told herself fiercely. He did it. He forced me to come with him, and that *is* kidnapping.

They were turning, approaching a marina lined with yachts and big sailboats, sleek, northern types. Two men in dark clothing were walking along one of the piers, looking at the boats. Even at this distance, she could see their heads turning, back and forth. She grew cold with anxiety. She could think of nothing except the old house at Fisherman's Cove, the painting that had glowed on the easel—and Jonathan in jail.

The Hideout was easing into a slip; she could hear Charlie's footsteps on the deck as he secured lines. They were docking in Nassau. She jumped from the chair and went out on the deck, ran forward and up into the saloon, up the steps to the flying bridge.

"I've got to tell you something," she said to Jonathan's startled stare. "Right now! Listen—call Max off. And if any strangers want to board this boat, you let them, do you hear? Because if you don't, you're going to be in trouble." She stopped because her voice was shaking and also because she could feel tears starting to well up in her eyes. She turned away and went down the steps, passing Rolf, who stood with the coffee pot in his hands staring at her in amazement. She walked on, eyes blurred, and found herself back in the lounge. She sat down, telling herself what a fool she was, and wiped her eyes angrily.

The door slid open and Jonathan came in, shutting it behind him and taking a chair next to hers.

"Do you mind telling me what that was all about?" His face wore an expression of warm interest; that was all.

"I sent a message," she said defiantly. "By now, or very soon, police will be searching for *The Hideout* to—

to take me off. Max would make them suspicious, and I want to keep your name out of it."

"In a case of kidnapping, you think you could keep my name out of it?" He laughed bitterly, incredulous. "Come off it, Lacey. I know you're smarter than that."

"I can. I'm going to show them my press credentials and tell them it was a put-up job—part of a series of articles I'm writing. Pike will back me up if I—" She stopped, staring at him. "You don't believe a word I'm saying, do you?"

"I believe it all," he said. "Every word." He stood up and plunged a hand into his pocket, brought forth a hundred-dollar bill and a torn piece of paper she recognized immediately. He dropped them both into her lap.

"I wondered why you told Madame Li not to mention my name," he said. "Now, I suppose I know."

She looked down at the bill and the note, shocked and disbelieving. They fluttered to the floor as she stood up and walked to a window, her face pale. "That—woman," she said, her back still toward him. "How could she do that to me?"

"Madame Li knows how to turn a profit," Jonathan said. "She waited for me beside my dinghy. I paid her considerably more than a hundred dollars to acquire these for myself and ensure that she did not make the call." He paused. "She also told me your instructions. I didn't see the point of keeping my name out of it. I would have thought you'd want revenge. Why did you try to protect me, Lacey?"

"Does it matter?" She couldn't bear to look at him, to see his triumph.

"It matters to me."

She shrugged. "I promised you once that I'd keep quiet about the old house where you paint. I thought, if you were mentioned, it might all come out."

She turned, startled, as his hands closed on her tense shoulders. He smiled down at her. "Is that all? If it hadn't been for your promise, you would have let them arrest me?"

He did look triumphant. She tore her gaze away from his eyes, fighting the familiar weakness. "A few days in jail might have shown you what it's like to lose your freedom," she said, "and you would have known how I feel." His arms were sliding around her, tightening, his head bending toward her, and she twisted her face away, only to find his warm mouth against her ear, sliding downward as he lifted her, coming to rest in the tender hollow of her shoulder. She gasped, and arched away from him. He laughed softly and let her slide down his body until her feet touched the floor again.

"I don't believe you would let them take me." He still held her, and he still looked triumphant. "But I wouldn't want to take the chance." His arms loosened, and his hands cupped her face. "You're a fighter; there's no doubt about that. Little and soft, maybe—but still a fighter." He bent quickly, lightly kissed her lips, then let her go. "Friends, I hope? I've got a suggestion that may help things..."

She turned away, still filled with emotion, with that feeling she hated to admit to herself. Her shoulder continued to burn where his lips had touched her flesh. "What's your suggestion?"

"Come on, I'll explain it over breakfast."

They walked out of the lounge into the middle of a stand-off. Charlie and Rolf, laughing but hesitant, were standing near the rail. Between them and the rail stood Max. The continuous low rumble coming from his chest, his lowered head, and his lifted lip made his intentions clear.

"Sorry!" This time, Jonathan was embarrassed. "Okay, Max. Good dog." He patted the Doberman as Max came to his side.

"Thanks a lot," Charlie said dryly. "We'd like to go ashore."

"Sure," Jonathan said quickly. "Sure, Charlie. Go ahead." He glanced at Lacey ruefully, and she burst into laughter, watching the two men leap to the dock and head toward land. "Somehow," she said, glancing up at him, "it's nice to know you aren't perfect."

"Nice to know you thought I was, up till now," he countered, his eyes narrowed against the sun. He took her hand. "Come on, we're wasting time."

In the saloon, they found a bowl of fruit, and a pot of coffee on the table, as well as warm Danish pastries in the oven. Over breakfast, Jonathan explained the arrangement he had in mind.

"You may not like it," he said, "because it means you can't go home yet." He shifted his weight on the bench to look at her directly. "There's something I haven't worked out yet, and until I do, I want you here. But I've decided that if you tell me you won't leave the island, won't call the States or give out any information at all, you can do whatever you like during the time we're here. Will you agree to that?"

Caught by surprise, she was silent. It was a great concession, she knew. Putting her on her honor when he believed she had lied to him from the start. A flash of insight told her that there was more at stake than just the privacy of the old house on Fisherman's Cove. Something new, maybe more important, maybe less. But something that had to be resolved here, not in New York or in Florida.

"Let me be sure I have it straight," she said. "If I don't leave and don't tell anyone anything, I can wander around alone. But I still have to live on the boat."

"Is that a hardship?"

"The accommodations are superb," she said lightly, "but at times the captain is rather overbearing." She watched his already bronzed face darken.

"I'll speak to him," he said.

She sighed and thought of alternatives. She was willing to bet that if she said no, she would never get to shore without a large hand on her arm, and so far all her attempts to escape her abductor had been futile. "You're offering me a short leash," she said finally. "But of course, I accept. I promise. A little freedom is better than none. But I hope you'll soon decide I'm not a real threat and let me go." She looked at him and saw the lingering doubt in his eyes. "Why did you decide to trust me, Jonathan?"

"Maybe because a promise seems to mean something to you. Maybe just because I want to." He got up, shoving his hands in the pockets of his white shorts, and leaned to peer through the porthole, looming larger than ever in the small space, like a man in a child's playhouse. When he turned back, a smile flashed on his shadowed face. "Let's forget our differences. I'll take you on your first sight-seeing trip. It's been a long time since I wandered this waterfront."

She was surprised at her own rush of pleasure. "Fine," she said, trying to keep her tone polite but no more. "Give me a few minutes to get ready, and I'll meet you on deck."

Through the cabin porthole, the sunlight held a hard brightness presaging a hot day. Lacey took off the rumpled pink top, brought out an apricot blouse of thin cotton that added gold to her beginning tan and set off the black satin of her hair. She dressed quickly, slipping her feet into sandals that were mere straps of white leather across her slim ankles and toes, thinking how well he had chosen for her, as if he had known precisely what would make her look her best, please her most. Leaving her cabin, she hunted up Cabot. Finding him stretched in the shade of the blue canvas at the stern, she picked him up and headed back toward the cabin. Jonathan, observing from his lounging position against the rail, looked surprised.

"Why shut him in?"

"He follows me," she said. "He won't obey like Max."

His eyes swept over her. "Who could blame him?"

"Flattery," she said, suddenly carefree. "I love it." On the deck, she took his arm, smiling up at him. The Bahamas. This would be a day to remember when this was all over.

* * *

Kisses Incognito

Unerringly, Jonathan took her where the exotic flavor of the island was most apparent. They strolled the quays where the out-islanders had unloaded. Amid the noise and confusion, they ate mangoes bought from the heaps of tropical fruit, peeled with Jonathan's pocket knife, juicy enough to make them lean forward warily while the golden liquid ran over their hands to drip on the stones. Laughing, untidy as children, they mopped up with tissues from her handbag. They strolled on, watching the live turtles swimming in tanks, the pink conchs squirming, the huge lobsters ready for sale. A constant bustle bombarding her ears, Lacey kept turning her head to see it all. The cries of fishermen advertising their wares wove a strident counterpoint to loud music that seemed to come from tiny alleys stretching away from the quays. She listened, feeling the wild drumbeat in her veins, until Jonathan noticed her absorbed look and smiled.

"Goombay," he said, "the Nassau version of calypso. Starts early and ends late, especially in the rum shops. There's even a sort of festival that celebrates it, like the New Orleans Mardi Gras. Except that this one seems to last all summer."

She followed in his wake through the growing crowd of tourists, of anxious fishermen vying for their dollars, and found that they were leaving the crush, entering a pleasant oval of neatly trimmed shrubbery, surrounded by a shopping center and a taxi stand, but dominated by what she knew had to be the famous Straw Market. The market had a bustle of its own, even so early, with vacationers filling the booths, intent on finding souvenirs. Lacey had been envying Jonathan the visored captain's hat that shaded his face; she glanced often at the wide-brimmed straw hats. Jonathan smiled and took her elbow, leading her toward a booth.

"Do you always know what I'm thinking?"

"Not always. But I'm working on it."

"Don't. I need privacy, too."

The sun grew hotter. The finely woven straw hat Jonathan had selected was cool on her thick black hair; the colors of the flowers that spilled across it complemented her apricot blouse. She was conscious of admiring glances from the thronging tourists pushing into the square. As Jonathan turned her toward the docks again, she thought of the air-conditioned lounge, the lunch of conch chowder Rolf had promised.

"This afternoon we'll go to Paradise," Jonathan said, "if you like."

She laughed. "How intriguing. Is Paradise around here?"

"It could be," he said, smiling, "but until we find out, we'll visit Paradise Island. There's a great beach for swimming."

They had reached the docks, and she took his arm. "It sounds lovely. But you must have seen it all before. Don't feel you have to—"

"I *want* to. I'll rent a car, and we'll take Max." He looked down at her. "Unless you... Do you mind?"

So he *couldn't* always read her thoughts. Lacey smiled. "I'd love it," she said carelessly, stepping over to the deck of *The Hideout*, seeing Charlie coming toward them. "I like guided tours."

"Randall was here," Charlie said, arriving. He gave Jonathan a glance that blended outrage and doubt. "He said it was important."

"He came *here?*" Jonathan looked suddenly grim, and Charlie glanced involuntarily at Lacey. "I'll tell you later..."

Hastily, Lacey walked on. In the lounge, she took off the new hat and stood in the cool current of the air conditioner, waiting. Jonathan came in, looked harried. "I have to leave for a while. Have your lunch and rest." His hand touched her shoulder and slid away, caressingly. "Mind waiting for me?"

"Not at all." She watched him leave, wondering why he was angry. He had been willing enough to meet Lance Randall before, on the ocean. She shrugged and sat down, leaning back, closing her eyes. The morning danced behind her eyelids. Jonathan watching her try on hats in the Straw Market, his eyes warm and teasing. Jonathan's arm across her back, protective as he took her through the crowds. Jonathan laughing. Jonathan's vivid blue eyes, crinkled, amused. She sat up, aware that it might be better if she broke her promise and fled to the nearest airport. She picked up a magazine and concentrated on it until Rolf served her a solitary lunch.

At three, Jonathan was back, striding down the dock. Charlie was waiting, and Lacey unabashedly listened from the lounge, catching some of their words.

"... more lies," Jonathan was saying, "but he swears it will work."

"He'll blow it." Charlie sounded disgusted, but Jonathan laughed.

"I'm beginning not to care."

Watching, Lacey saw him coming toward the lounge and sat down again, smiling as he came in.

"Be right with you," he said, and headed for his cabin, returning in seconds wearing snug blue trunks and carrying beach towels.

"Where's your bathing suit?"

In answer, she stood up and whirled around. The lime-green pareo floated away, exposing the silver-lilac suit. While changing clothes, she had seen that the silk-screened orchids on the pareo were also lilac, and had wondered if the color coordination had been deliberate or merely fortuitous. Either way, the combination was perfect, the pareo a perfect covering for the revealing one-piece suit. "Do I need more?"

"Sandals," Jonathan said. "There's a trail to the beach."

She went to get them, happiness bubbling inside her like champagne. She would worry later about forgetting him.

Chapter 8

ONLY THE BRIDGE proved Paradise Island an island. Otherwise, it seemed of a piece with Nassau, bustling with crowds, host to a gambling casino, golf courses, tennis courts. But once they were on the trail to the beach, the tropical flavor returned. Cool and green, the trail wound through a grove of casuarina trees, brightened by red hibiscus blossoms. Max strained at his leash, pulling them forward through the departing crowd.

"We're late," Jonathan said, smiling, as a group pushed past them, sand-covered and laughing, carrying their portable radios and foam coolers. "We'll have the beach to ourselves." He caught her around the waist as they reached the opening onto the beach. "Look! What do you think of it?"

A crescent of white sand, a glistening sweep of clear blue water. Thatched huts for shade and giant coconut palms that leaned from the trade winds. Lacey ran, the pareo fluttering. She stopped to take off her sandals, then ran on until her feet were caught in the whispering curl of a wave. Eventually, she turned and ran back to where Jonathan was spreading beach towels.

"A South Sea island," she said, breathless, her hands busy with the knot of the pareo.

"South Atlantic," he amended, watching her toss the pareo on a towel, then straighten, slim but deliciously curved in the skintight, shimmering lilac suit. He dropped

Max's leash. "Stay," he said to the dog, and took Lacey's hand.

"Lorelei," he whispered, "temptress of the sea. Come on, I'll take you to your natural element."

They plunged through waves to deeper, calmer water and swam. After the tension of the last few days, the freedom and buoyancy made the clear water like wine to Lacey. She played, swimming under water, somersaulting in the depth with languid grace, coming up to float, watching the sky dreamily. Rising below her, Jonathan grasped her waist with both hands and raised her on his head like a tumbler. She screamed, and he silently submerged, leaving her floating again. She laughed and turned over, her face in the water, watching his bronzed body below, his broad mouth trailing silver bubbles, his hands gesturing to her. She dived toward him, and he caught her, pulling her close. They rose together, legs entwined, to the surface. Lacey burst into laughter, her pewter eyes shining, starred with water clinging to her long lashes.

"You were a seductive merman," she said. "No woman could resist you!" She pushed away from him to swim again, and he pulled her back.

"Then don't resist," he said dramatically. "Stay, my earthly beauty. I'll show you treasures in the deep..." Slowly, he pulled her with him beneath the surface again, their bodies sliding sinuously together, sinking to the bottom. When she pushed against him, he let her go, rose after her. Face solemn, he handed her a rosy piece of broken shell. "Not much of a treasure," he said, "but I really enjoyed the trip."

"Sensational," she said shakily, "and the treasure is nice, too." She was warm from the rush of excitement she had felt, held to his nearly naked body, aware that she wanted him more than ever. She forced herself to turn and swim away from him, but when he followed and put a possessive arm across her waist, she moved toward him to be held again.

The shadows of the big palm trees were long on the

gleaming sand when they walked back up to their towels, streaming water, panting. Max lay with his long jaws resting on his forelegs, his eyes mournful.

"We forgot him," Lacey said, penitent. "How sad he looks. You promised him exercise, remember?" She leaned and picked up the Doberman's leash, then tugged. Max rolled his eyes at Jonathan, who laughed and said the words that released him.

Max was on his feet, wriggling, happy. Lacey tugged again. "Come on," she said. "We'll run." She set off down the nearly deserted beach with the dog, running on bright sand and through the long tree shadows, the slim feminine figure and big Doberman alternately shining and dimming as they went, turning far away to come back. She turned once and saw Jonathan watching them, the towel he had picked up forgotten in his hand.

"Here," she said, panting to a stop, handing him the leash. "He's—he's exercised. And I am, too..." Her voice trailed away as she was caught by his gaze. She stood, lips parted in her flushed face, her breasts heaving after the run, drowning in the sea blue of his eyes. When he dropped the leash and reached for her, she went into his arms as if she were going home, accepting his deep kiss, her arms tight around him, her hands moving, caressing, on his bare back.

It was a kiss that gave everything, asked for everything. His lips slid from her mouth, coursed fire across her cheek and down the slender column of her neck. Muffled in the soft curve of her shoulder, his voice was hoarse. "You are so very beautiful..."

Eyes closed, her body tight against his, she knew her resistance had melted like snow on this tropic beach. Her blood sang; his kisses had turned her heart inside out. And she didn't care. Why not surrender, have it all—even though it couldn't last? The memory might last forever. She drew back from him, met his passionate gaze with soft gray eyes. "Let's go home," she said, her lips curving, "before we shock the natives."

Towels bundled in their arms, Max dragging his loose

leash, they ran up the beach and into the green avenue. There they slowed and walked, silent, Jonathan's arm around her waist. It was late, the sun slanted low through the casuarinas, laying bars of gold across the path. Before they emerged from the shelter of the trees, he stopped and kissed her again, questioning her with his eyes as if he could not believe what was happening. By the time they started on, Max had tired of dragging his leash and picked it up in his teeth; he walked before them with his head high, the loop swinging, and waited patiently for Jonathan to open the car door.

It seemed unreal. The joyous certainty Lacey had felt on the beach dissolved on the yacht. The presence of Charlie and Rolf shocked her into instant sanity, and she hurried below to shower. Washing the salt from her hair, she toweled it dry in front of a small mirror that reflected back the image of her bare breasts. Pink tips were matched by a vee of sun-pinked skin between them, and she thought it looked ludicrous. Yet he expected... he was sure... She turned from the mirror, her body flooded helplessly with warm weakness. It was scary to think of giving him that ultimate power over her...

The turquoise pareo hung on a hook on the bathroom door. She put it on, knotted it tightly, her heart jumping at the sound of footsteps in her cabin. Her hand shaking, she pushed back her damp hair and opened the door.

He was standing by the porthole, looking out, dressed only in white shorts. He had turned on the small lamp beside the door, the light glowed on his bronze shoulders, made shadows along the muscles of his back. He turned and looked at her, smiling faintly.

"We have asked for a late supper," he said, "because we are very tired. Rolf has left it for us, and he and Charlie have gone ashore for the night."

Looking at him, hearing the caressing tenderness in his deep voice, she was suddenly, joyously, certain again. She laughed softly, her eyes sparkling silver. "And, are we hungry?"

"*I* am." He closed the distance between them with a

long stride, his arms circling her waist, his eyes intent on hers. "Are you?"

"Starved," she said, and slid her palms up his broad chest, locking her slim fingers behind his neck, rocked by the pervading male warmth penetrating the thin silk of the pareo. Her breath caught in her throat as his arms tightened suddenly, dragging her against him in a surge of dominating male passion, his mouth hot on hers, demanding... Then, just as suddenly, he made a deep, inarticulate sound and loosened his arms. He looked down at her, his eyes vulnerable.

"Lord," he said hoarsely, "what's the matter with me? Don't let me rush this, please." His lips touched her eyes, trailed down her cheek to brush her mouth. "It has to be loving, darling... slow and sweet. It has to be wonderful for us both..."

Shaken, Lacey sighed and leaned against him, her face in the hollow of his shoulder. "It will be," she murmured, holding him, her hands stroking his back, tracing the muscles beneath the warm skin. "It will be beautiful." Her lips still tingled from his hard kiss as she looked up. "Won't it?"

"Yes." He leaned to kiss her again, his mobile mouth moving slowly, sensually across her softening lips, his tongue beginning a teasing flicker, sliding in quick invasions against the sensitive corners.

"Lovely," she said against his lips. "Do more..." She was homing in on the sensation, her arms going around his neck, her own tongue beginning to curl coaxingly, wanting the full, deep thrust to possess her. When it came, she pulled his head down, their mouths and bodies welded together, swaying, hot with the first promise of mating. Breathless, she finally pulled away. "That," she said, panting, "was more... and more."

"Never enough." His hand had slipped through the folds of the pareo, found its way to the silky skin of her back, moved in gentle circles over her slender waist. "Look at me, Lacey."

Molded to his body, she looked up and met his eyes,

knowing he must see in her gaze what she saw in his—a dark velvet passion, a wanting... Her breathing sharpened as his hand moved, unseen beneath the loose silk, pushed between them to caress her smooth belly. Then it slid slowly upward, to lie, warm and still, between her full breasts. She felt the nipples tighten in exquisite pain, the breasts expanding, and she closed her eyes, breathing deeply, waiting...

"*Look* at me." His voice was tender, compelling, and she opened her eyes again. He held her gaze, his own eyes deep blue and intense, penetrating, as if he could see far within her, see each flicker of flame, every jolt of desire. It was deeply erotic, and she kept her eyes on his, wanting him to see how she felt as his hands began to move, closing strongly over the swelling flesh, kneading, teasing the tight nipples with his rough palm, moving back and forth, over and over, while he held her darkening eyes, watching her lips open in soundless gasps, the tip of her tongue slowly moisten them.

His breathing had changed. His body against hers was wild with arousal, the hand on her breasts hot and tight. "Lacey, darling, your eyes are burning me up." His hand left her abruptly, and he swung her into his arms, turning toward the bed, hugging her close before he put her down in the nest of pillows. Dropping to sit on the sea of white ruffles, he leaned forward and kissed her. "That look," he said, his voice still ragged, "should be illegal."

His fingers were untying the knot of the pareo, sliding the folds from beneath her, tossing the limp silk aside. His hands went to her bare breasts, encircling the ivory and pink mounds tenderly. "Along with these," he added, and leaned to take a nipple, sucking it into his mouth, rolling it with his rough tongue, leaving it wet and glistening in the lamplight as he went to the other. Lacey let out her breath and sank back, pulling him with her, pressing her breast into his mouth, her fingers tugging in his hair. Her whole body was responding, moving in supple rhythm, curling toward him.

He trailed a line of kisses up her neck, across her

cheek. "I'm going to love every inch of you." His husky promise fanned warm breath on her mouth, and he moved away, slipping off his shorts, then stretching out on the bed to hold her, one hand exploring, his gaze traveling along her body like a caress that warmed where it touched.

Her body gleamed in the faint glow of the lamp, the mounds of her breasts high and tight, the curves of her waist and thighs shadowed, his dark hand a deeper shadow on her creamy skin. A shadow that kneaded and teased tantalizingly, that crept like living fire over her tingling skin. Watching his hand through half-closed eyes, she trembled with desire and looked away, pressing her face into his neck, conscious that his scent had changed subtly, had become deliciously warm and musky, seductive... Her mouth opened, tasting, her tongue softly caressing as she felt the hand smooth down the curve of hip and thigh, flattening warmly on her belly, searching out secrets in the dusky triangle of tight black curls. Then it had slipped between her soft inner thighs, finding the velvety womanly folds and drawing a tender, slow path through them, smoothing upward to feather around the sensitive apex of desire.

Moans rose in her throat, low, husky sounds, and she turned to touch him, her mouth following her hands as they moved over him. Slowly, she traced with fingers and lips the column of his neck, the line of broad shoulder. Down the taut taper of his side, her mouth trailing heat, biting gently, her fingers smoothing his hard flanks, around his flat belly, and up his broad chest, sliding through the mat of crisp hair, her mouth finding his again as she curved into him, thighs pressing softly against hard male passion. She was on fire, rippling with flame, her body moving sinuously, caressing his. She felt the plunging beat of his blood as he groaned and moved over her.

"Now, darling."

"Yes... yes, now."

He was careful of his weight on her slim body, entering slowly, tense with the holding back. But when she thrust upward to enclose him completely and began a pressing, sensual movement of her own, he took her with hard, deep thrusts that swept them both with aching desire, drove them deep into a warm and fluid passion that blotted out thought. Then the jolting, ecstatic throbbing began in her, fiery waves rolling out from his thrusts, beating like drums as he groaned and pulsed hard within her. Spent, they clung together and floated up from darkness as they had in the warm sea. She opened her eyes and found his gaze on her face, his mouth tender.

"Lorelei," he whispered, and laughed, rolling over on his back, pulling her with him, raising her until his face rested between her breasts.

"How," he said indistinctly, "could anything be quite that wonderful?" He sat up, still holding her, smiling at her half-closed, still dreamy eyes. "Lacey," he murmured, "you've changed my life. And I never thought anyone could do that."

She smiled, tracing his thick brows with a fingertip. "Don't change, Jonathan... Never change."

Later, eating lobster salad in the saloon, he told her he was leaving in the early morning. "I have to do something," he said. "I've put it off too long. I may be gone two or three days."

She looked at him questioningly, and he shook his head. "I'm not the only one involved," he said, "and it's confidential. But you'll be the first to know when it's over."

She drifted off to sleep in his arms that night, feeling the even rise and fall of his heavy chest against her, reveling in the big, protective body curled around hers. Waking, chilled, in the blackness before dawn, she knew he was gone. She pulled the blanket up and lay wondering. Something he had put off too long. She hoped suddenly that it meant he would be breaking off whatever connection he had with Lance Randall. There was something wrong, there... something that made her uneasy.

Chapter 9

HE HAD LEFT her a sealed note, with her name on the envelope. Inside, a page in strong but graceful script: "Lorelei, have fun while I'm gone. Why don't you take a tour? The guides are good here, and you'll be safe. J. P. S. Thanks for the preview of heaven."

She looked up and smiled at Charlie, who had just returned with Rolf. Charlie's graying hair was ruffled by the morning breeze. "He must have left early," she said noncommittally.

Charlie nodded. "He took Max, I guess. Does the note say where he went?"

"No." She stared at Charlie thoughtfully. "Why would he take Max?"

"Always does if he's going to be gone more than one day," Charlie said gruffly, "but I wish he hadn't... The cat's hunting him already. That cat is crazy."

"Everyone says so," Lacey said wearily, "so I guess he must be. I'll find him." She left, walking aft, lonely already. A guided tour. Shuffling along in a crowd, listening to the mechanical, singsong patter. Ugh.

Cabot was sitting alone under the blue canvas awning at the stern, staring at the dock with his ears flat.

"So, now you don't like docks," she said, picking him up and stroking him. "Max must have left on those boards. Never mind. Maybe I'll bark for you, occasionally." She turned and saw Rolf behind her, leaning on the rail, his tanned young face breaking up into laughter.

"Sort of a one-sided conversation, isn't it?"

"Better than none," Lacey said, "better than taking a guided tour, too. That's what I'm supposed to do today."

"Hey, those tours are good," Rolf said, surprising her. "You learn a lot. The guide tells you what's important."

Lacey laughed, amused by his serious look. "Then why don't you go with me? It's more fun with someone along."

Rolf flushed. "You mean that?"

"Certainly. You can even pick the tour."

"The fort, then," he said immediately. "It's great. But you haven't had your breakfast yet."

"Don't rush me," Lacey said dryly. "With a tour to look forward to, I want to savor the anticipation."

"I loved those gloomy dungeons," Lacey said, "and the staircases spiraling down, down..." They were leaving Fort Charlotte, Rolf's hand on her arm as he escorted her back to the surrey he had hired. "Think," she added, "how you'd feel if you were an enemy prisoner being led, chained and clanking, down those steps." She laughed. "Not that any ever were. Did you read the plaque? Never a shot fired in anger. No fights at all."

"Look at it this way," Rolf said, handing her into the surrey, "they never lost a battle." Under the breeze-whipped, silver-blond hair, his hazel eyes sparkled as he climbed in beside her.

"Queen Street," he said to the driver, "and then the Queen's Staircase." As the driver nodded and started the old horse again, Rolf put his arm along the back of the seat, leaning close. "Fort Charlotte was named for a queen, too. It all seems right for you, princess."

His young, eager face was very close. Lacey twisted in the seat to face him, putting distance between them.

"Thank you. This must be the royal treatment. When do we join the guided tour?"

Rolf laughed. "We're on it. I'm the guide and you're the guidee." He caught her hand and held it. "I've wanted to get you alone ever since I first saw you. You're so lovely, Lacey. When I saw you in those white shorts . . ."

"Sh-h-h." She glanced at the driver pointedly and then, surprised, back at Rolf. His arm had slid from the seat to her shoulders and was drawing her close. "Rolf!"

"Oh, all right. I don't want to rush you." He sat back, still clutching her hand. "You're supposed to look at these houses; they're famous. Most of them are around two hundred years old. Aren't the balconies great?"

She looked at the old houses, the graceful balconies, the flowers—oleander, hibiscus, trailing bougainvillaea. A breathtaking sight, but difficult to appreciate while dealing with Rolf's sudden ardor. "Beautiful," she said politely.

"So are you," Rolf said enthusiastically. "When Jon sends you home, may I camp on your doorstep?"

When Jon sends you home. The words echoed in her ears and slid down to the pit of her stomach. She pulled her hand from Rolf's. "Oh, look," she said, "we're leaving Queen Street. What did you say was next?"

"The staircase," Rolf said, "and what makes it remarkable is . . ."

She leaned back, not listening, as the horse trotted on, sweat glistening on its thin flanks, a straw hat with perky flowers bobbing on its head. The old man who drove kept his eyes forward. They clopped along until the Queen's Staircase came into view, the dark stone steps rising, fountains shooting high beside them. The old man stopped the horse and in a moment turned to look at them, puzzled because they were still sitting in the surrey, staring at a group of people near the fountains."

"You want to get out, miss?"

"What? Oh, no! No, I don't." She looked at Rolf urgently. "Could we go?"

"Certainly. Take us back to the docks." His voice was quick, assertive, and the driver responded automatically, turning the surrey with uncharacteristic speed. Lacey shrank back, glad for Rolf's fast reaction, glad for his shoulders, which hid her from the group by the fountains.

It couldn't be Rick Lonigan, but it was. Standing there chatting with another man, almost hidden by the people around him, he had thrown back his head and laughed, and her memory had taken her back a year. Why was he here? Had he somehow found out where Jonathan was? Or, finding himself in Florida with nothing to do, had he decided on a few days' vacation in the islands? Either way, he was dangerous. She looked up and found Rolf gazing at her, concerned.

"Are you all right?"

She took a deep breath, resisting the impulse to turn and look behind them. "Yes. I mean, no, not really. I felt a little dizzy—but I think it's wearing off."

"The sun," Rolf said. "Some people can't take it. We'll go back to the boat, and you can lie down. I'll fix you an ice bag."

"Thank you. That sounds like just what I need," she said. And, meaning it, she added, "You are really kind."

He smiled, coloring. "It's easy for me to be kind to you."

She sat up and took another deep breath, moving slightly away from him. "I think I should tell you," she said, "that—well, there's someone else..." The words sounded strange to her ears, and rather wonderful, except that she thought he might know immediately who the someone was, and that would prove embarrassing. But still she had to warn him off.

Rolf stared out from under the fringed canopy of the surrey with a rather theatrical look of suffering. "I should have known," he said. "A woman like you always has someone." He smiled stiffly. "I'll bet he misses you."

"I hope so," Lacey said. "I miss him."

The next day she spent on the boat, trying to read, sitting in the lounge. She looked carefully around outside before she ventured on deck, made quick trips to the saloon and back. By afternoon, she decided she was acting paranoid. If Rick had learned that Jonathan was here on a boat, he would have searched every marina by now. He would not have missed a single detail. But this time, he was going to be disappointed. There was no unknown genius painting while Jonathan took the credit. And, even if he saw Jonathan here, he wouldn't know about the old house on the cove. There was nothing to connect Jonathan with Tarpon City... except her!

Her heart sank. She picked up her book and stared at it, unseeing. The very best thing she could do for Jonathan now was to go home. And that was the very last thing she wanted to do.

There was a scrabbling sound at one of the windows, startling her. She turned quickly. Two large paws, a long black and tan head with red tongue panting over white teeth, dark eyes gleaming. Springing to her feet, she went to open the door, and Max bounded in, bumped her with his nose, circled her twice, and stood quivering as she stroked him.

"I think you've stolen my dog." Jonathan was looming in the doorway, relaxed and smiling, his electric blue eyes searching her face. Her heart somersaulted and began to thump. She looked away from him to Max, her fingers rubbing the hollow behind the Doberman's ear. Max leaned against her contentedly.

"Cabot missed him," she said, and thought how inconsequential that sounded. "Why do you say I've stolen him?"

"He beat me down the dock, looking for you," Jon said, and came to her, tipping up her face with long fingers. "Rolf said you didn't feel well. True?"

It all came back, and she stepped away from him. "I told Rolf that story as an excuse to return to the boat," she said. "Rick Lonigan is here on the island. I didn't want him to spot me."

She had expected an explosion, but it didn't happen. His expression sharpened but he didn't look surprised. "You've seen him?"

She nodded and explained rapidly. "I didn't see Marla with him," she ended, "so I don't know if she's here.

He was with a man I couldn't see well—light-haired, not as tall as Rick..."

"Lonigan didn't see you?"

"No. I—hid behind Rolf." She flushed, thinking about it. "We were in a surrey, sight-seeing."

His grin was tight. "Lucky Rolf," he commented dryly. He turned to pace a few steps away from her, wheeled, and came back. "It might be better if we got away from Nassau for a day or so. I've been worried about this happening."

"You knew Rick was here?"

"Yes. Marla Pomeroy, too." At her sudden shocked look, he added, "It's all right—part of a plan..." He opened the door, looking down at Max. "Go find the cat," he said. "We need some privacy in here." Obediently, Max left her side and went out.

"Now," he said, moving toward her, "come here. Max isn't the only one who missed you." He caught her as she took an involuntary step backward. His arms went around her, and his mouth was gentle but insistent on hers. For a moment, she yielded, clinging to him in a rush of breathless hunger, her lips softly accepting. Then, as his kiss deepened, she dropped her arms and stepped away abruptly.

"You live dangerously," she said. "What if your fiancée happens to drop in? Since she's in Nassau, she may be looking for *The Hideout*."

His look of surprise was followed by a grin. "You forget, darling. She's not my fiancée."

She looked up at his remembering eyes, at his mouth, and decided that the statement was one she would be glad to believe. She put her hands on his chest and slid them slowly up to circle his neck. "She thinks she is," she said, "but that's only her opinion..." She pulled his head down, stopping their laughter with a kiss, fitting her body tightly to his.

After a long moment, he relaxed his hold. "Careful. You'll make me forget everything—and I think it's important that we leave. I don't want Lonigan to see you."

She nodded, stepping out of the circle of his arms, pushing her hair away from her warm face. "I know. I thought of that and stayed out of sight. I'm the connection to the old house. It would be better to hide me. If he catches sight of me, he'll know I met you in the vicinity of Fisherman's Cove." She looked at him, stricken. "The safest move of all would be to send me home," she added slowly. "I know you trust me, now."

"No! I'm not letting you go. There's something I can do that could settle the whole question. I want you with me until I work it all out. Then we'll see where we go from there." He flung himself into a chair, his brows drawn down. "As far as the place at the cove goes, that problem may be solved."

She sat beside him. "How?"

"Lance dreamed this whole thing up for me," he said, less than satisfied. "He invited Rick and Marla here. He called her father in New York and got her telephone number. Then he told her and Lonigan that he had decided to show them the secret studio where Grey's paintings originated." He smiled faintly. "He has a secluded house with a studio in it, out near Gambier, right here on New Providence. He put my new paintings around and took Lonigan and Marla out to see it. He's sure he has Lonigan convinced."

"Wonderful!" Lacey leaned forward. "If Rick is satisfied, he'll stop looking. So that's where you were yesterday—playing host to the two of them." She laughed. "I hope you had a brush in your hand, a little paint here and there..."

He shook his head, avoiding her eyes. "*I* wasn't there. Not when they came. I didn't want to see either of them. I helped Lance get the studio ready. We hung the paintings, set up an easel. It's a good studio; it wasn't hard to make it look authentic."

"If Rick didn't find you there, he won't quit," she said, her voice flat with disappointment. "What he wants most is to prove you're a fake. You'll have to show him you're not before he gives up that idea."

"A fake? What do you mean?" He was suddenly tense, she noticed, and trying to hide it.

"Didn't I tell you? No, I know I didn't. It wasn't important, once I knew it wasn't true. Rick's got a crazy idea that you don't paint—that you have an unknown artist doing the paintings for you." She laughed. "It's ridiculous, I know. But all you have to do is show up there at the studio and prove to him..." She stopped, her voice trailing away, watching his thick brows draw together, his jaw set hard.

"So that's it. I've been wondering why Lonigan thought the story warranted so much attention." Jonathan sprang up from his chair and strode to the window, staring out. "I'll have to go back," he added slowly, and swung back to face her. "I wanted to be with you..." He bent over and kissed her lingeringly. "I'll be back by morning, darling. Be thinking about that trip."

Standing at the window, she watched him leave. He stopped on deck and talked to Charlie, gave Max a pat and a hand signal that meant stay, and then he was gone, striding quickly. Lacey went back to her chair and flung herself down again. She supposed he would go to the house near Gambier and arrange to have Lance bring Rick and Marla there again. Perhaps he would pretend to be painting. Maybe he would give Rick an interview in his secret hideaway on the island of New Providence. It would be all pretense, lies. It was more like Rick than it was like the Jonathan she knew. Covering up with deceit and falseness.

Still, she thought, she had seen enough in New York to know how the public hounded celebrities. She realized what it would be like if everyone knew about the old house and where it was. It would be a mark of prestige in name-dropping circles to be able to say casually that you'd been to Grey's quaint old place and had actually seen him painting.

And the media. She thought wryly that at one time she would have been the first to push in, bring a photographer, demand an interview and pictures.

Rick would be disappointed tonight. His appetite for sensational scandal was insatiable, and he wanted very much to be able to expose Jonathan Grey as a fake. And since he was almost always right when he went in for the kill, discovering he was wrong would make him furious. She knew from experience that when Rick was angry he turned rapidly from charming to vindictive. The thought was frightening, and she got up. It was almost time for dinner, and she felt rumpled and in need of a shower.

Even though she would be dining alone, she dressed with care, and it improved her feelings enormously. She wore the flame-colored pareo for the first time, draping it in the easiest way by wrapping it simply from front to back and then drawing the glowing fabric ends evenly to the front and tying them in the tiniest of knots. The soft drapery outlined her body seductively, fluttered as she walked. The gold chain around her neck matched the golden orchids painted on the flowing ends of the pareo, and she had washed her hair so that it shone like ebony above the flame. She left her mirrored wall with the feeling that she looked her best, and with a small regret that Jonathan wasn't around to see her. Nevertheless, she felt light and carefree as she walked through the lounge and stepped out on the deck.

"Beautiful," Rick Lonigan said, lounging easily on the pier beside the boat. "In fact, I've never seen you looking better."

As shock receded, memories assailed her. His alert and cynical face was so familiar, with the wayward lock of brown hair that always hung over one of his wing-shaped eyebrows. She knew so well that twisted, humorous mouth, the slanted, knowing eyes. He was still amazingly attractive in his own way. Even his angular body had a peculiar grace, hesitating now on the edge of the pier, ready to step onto the deck beside her.

He watched her, and she knew he had counted on the shock value. He knew she was off-balance, remembering. "Mind if I come aboard, Lacey?"

"I mind," she said, and looked desperately along the deck. Max was lying near the saloon steps, and she spoke to him without thinking about it at all. "Guard, Max."

The Doberman's long head turned to her in momentary surprise, and then he was bounding toward her, turning to the rail, muscles bunching as he lowered his head and looked at Rick, rumbling a deep warning. Lacey laughed, unable to stop. She had never before seen Rick Lonigan frightened.

"Good Lord," he said, stepping backward slowly, his eyes on the dog's lifted lip, the long white teeth. "You really do mind." His eyes came back to her full of a reluctant respect, a beginning anger. "What's the problem? Afraid an old boyfriend might irritate your lover?" A sound from the saloon steps caught his attention, and he stared, the twisted smile appearing again. "He looks a bit young, Lacey."

Rolf was coming toward them, his tanned face troubled and suspicious, looking from Lacey to the stranger on the dock and, with surprise, at the dog. Lacey smiled.

"Not at all," she said sweetly. "We're about the same age." She went to Rolf, put her arm in his, and turned him back toward the steps. Over her shoulder, she added: "Good-bye, Rick. The pier, of course, is public. Perhaps you would like to continue your conversation with the dog." Signaling Rolf with the pressure of her hand, she led him up the steps and into the saloon.

Inside, Rolf pulled loose from her grasp. "Who is he?" he asked. "And why is he here?" He didn't look particularly young at the moment.

She collapsed on the bench and put her elbows on the table, burying her head in her hands. She let out her breath in a long sigh.

"Rick Lonigan," she said. "Does the name mean anything to you?"

"Not much," he said after a pause. "I've read his

column once or twice, but I didn't care for it. What is he doing here?"

It wasn't for her to tell him if Jonathan hadn't. "I—I guess he's looking for me," she said. "He used to be a friend of mine."

Rolf sat down heavily on the bench opposite her. "What kind of friend?" He stared at her with disapproval. "A close friend? A good friend?"

"Too close," she said levelly. "And not good at all. I haven't seen him in over a year, and I don't want to see him now."

"Great. He's way too old for you."

She laughed helplessly, leaning back against the cushioned bench. "That's the least of his faults," she said. "Anyway, I didn't even want to talk to him."

Rolf grinned for the first time since they had come in. "I guess you didn't. You set Max on him. Lonigan will probably never forgive you for that."

She stopped laughing and looked at him soberly. "You're right. He never will. And he'll do his best to get even." She leaned back again and shut her eyes, feeling the reaction of fright and anger, wondering how much Rick knew, or had guessed. If she was right, he would be seeing Jonathan this evening. It was impossible to imagine what he might do or say. She sat up. Jonathan could handle it. It would be all right.

Rolf had left the table; now he was back and pouring white wine into a stemmed glass for her. "Shrimp again," he said cheerily. "Think you can stand it?"

"I'll love it," she said gratefully. "Where's Charlie?"

"I've been wondering myself," Rolf said, back in the galley and stirring energetically. "He went to town for some pipe tobacco at least an hour ago. It's not like him to miss dinner."

"It's a pleasant evening," Lacey said comfortably, sipping her wine. "Maybe he just—Oh!" She leaped to her feet and ran out, her pareo fluttering, her stricken glance searching the dock. Rick Lonigan was gone, but Charlie looked back at her grimly from his seat on the edge of the dock. Max wagged his short tail at the sound of her footsteps, but his warning eyes never left Charlie.

"I'm sorry—really sorry," Lacey wailed, flying down the companionway. "Okay, Max. Good dog." She dropped her head to hide a smile as the Doberman came wriggling toward her, bumping her bare ankle with his nose, standing to be petted.

Charlie, climbing stiffly over the rail, did not appear to find the incident humorous.

"I can explain," Lacey said, a trifle wildly. "At least, I hope I can..."

Chapter 10

THE LEVEL OF the bed shifted, waking Lacey into darkness. She yawned, waiting for the inevitable tilt to the other side, wondering at the strength of a night wind that would rock the boat in the protected marina. Then a finger traced the curve of her cheek, and she shot into a sitting position, stifling the cry that rose in her throat. But the dark shape on the bed beside her was somehow fully recognizable. She dropped back into Jonathan's arms, finding his chest, bare and warm, with its scattering of crisp hair.

"You're lucky I didn't scream the place down," she said, trying to sound displeased. "What would you have said if Charlie and Rolf had burst in and found you here, naked?"

"That you tempted me with your siren song and I was helplessly drawn to you," he said gravely. "What else would you have me do but tell the truth?"

She buried her face in his neck, hiding her laughter, then grew serious as his hand slipped beneath the sheet, exploring.

"Why are you wearing a nightgown?"

"To sleep in."

"But you're not sleeping," he said reasonably. His hand was gathering up the folds of silky material, his fingers brushing the soft flesh of her thighs. When he had the gown bunched around her hips, he sat up, pulling her with him, lifting her, and whisked the gown off over her head. "A delicate thing," he said, tossing it aside. "Too fragile to stand the wear it would get in the next few hours."

"Hours?"

"Certainly." He fell backward into the rumpled bed, holding her, so that she lay across his body. She saw the white flash of his grin. "If you persist in haunting me every minute I'm away, then you have to take the consequences."

"I'm quite willing," she said primly, and bent her head to kiss him, teasing his broad mouth with the tip of her tongue, feeling her heart begin its slow pounding, the familiar warm weakness spreading, the sweet ache in her loins. She took her mouth from his and slid to the bed beside him, closing her eyes as he turned to begin his slow, sweet possession. Bittersweet—knowing how short a time she would be with him. She had to gather enough memories to last a lifetime during these few days... and nights.

He left in the dim glow of first light, gathering up the clothes he had strewn on the floor, leaning to kiss her warm, sleepy face. "I'll rouse the crew," he whispered. "I've got plans." He was gone before she could ask any questions. She drifted back to sleep and was startled later by a peremptory knock on her door.

"What is it?"

"Meet me in the saloon in five minutes," came Jonathan's voice, taut and displeased. She scrambled from the bed and dressed quickly, wondering.

"Suppose you tell me about it from the beginning." Jonathan's eyes, looking at her across the table littered with the remains of his breakfast and the beginning of hers, seemed to hold a cool restraint.

"It's just as Rolf told you," Lacey said, sipping coffee. The knock had wakened her from a sound sleep. It was still only six-thirty, and her head felt fuzzy. She wished he had let her wake up naturally. "Rick showed up and wanted to come aboard to talk to me, and I gave Max the command to guard. That's all that happened, really." She looked at his stiff face and bit her lip. "It's bad luck he found us, I know. I suppose I should have talked to him—found out what he knew..."

"No. You were right not to discuss anything with him. The less he knows right now, the better. But I still want to know what he said." The sea-blue eyes bored into hers. "He had to say something, Lacey. Start with 'hello' and perhaps you'll remember the rest."

"I'd have to start with 'Beautiful,'" Lacey said, thinking back. "That's the first thing he said. And then he said, 'In fact, I've never seen you looking better.'"

"Wonderful dialogue," Jonathan said, his broad mouth flattening. "And then, I suppose, you said, 'Oh, thank you, it's so nice of you to say so.'"

"I didn't thank him. I suppose that was rude of me. I didn't say anything, right then." She was still thoughtful. "But he did. He asked me if I minded if he came aboard. I said I minded. Then I saw Max lying on the deck, and I told him to guard, just the way you do." She smiled. "He did it, too. It scared Rick, and I'm afraid I laughed. Then Rolf came out on deck, and Rick thought he was my boyfriend. I let him think so, and took Rolf's arm and left. And—oh, yes, I did tell him something— I told him the dock was public and he could stay and talk to the dog. I don't think he stayed long, though, because Charlie said later that Rick was gone when he came back—" She stopped, remembering what had occurred when Charlie came back.

"So Charlie said," Jonathan observed, his eyes glinting. "I find it hard to believe that Max would obey your commands. He's supposed to be my dog."

She looked at him over her coffee cup and then set it down. "You told me once that my cat was smarter than I was. Maybe your dog is smarter than you are."

His thick brows shot up. "You mean Max knows instinctively that you're completely on my side? I wish I thought so. As it is, I wonder. I know you saw Lonigan when you went ashore with Rolf. But have you seen him again, away from the boat?"

Her gray eyes changed, growing smoky. "I can't imagine you having to ask me that, now," she said through clenched teeth.

He grabbed her arm as she jumped to her feet. "Sit down. I only asked because I know you had—had a relationship with him. I keep thinking that maybe you still have some feelings for him. Talking to him, you might have let something slip. And it's important he doesn't know anything—yet." He tugged her arm. "Please, sit down."

"No!" She twisted her arm from his grasp. "I've had enough coffee and more than enough of *you*." She left, fired by anger, and ran down the companionway. In her cabin, she whirled and locked the door before flinging herself on the frilly bed. He actually thought she would sneak away and talk to Rick while he was gone! And be stupid enough to "let something slip." Didn't he *know* how she felt about him? But then, she thought, growing calmer, maybe it's a good thing he doesn't...

It didn't matter, anyway. All this running back and forth had to mean that Jonathan and Lance Randall were working things out together. Soon she would be back at *The Clarion,* writing about weddings and bingo games. Or would she? There were other places she could go...

She was brushing her hair when she felt the vibration, heard the rumble of the engines. It startled her, after the silence at the dock. She put the brush down and went to look out the porthole. Two familiar figures, their backs to the sea, were walking briskly along the rapidly receding pier, each carrying a tightly strapped nylon suitcase. Charlie and Rolf. She jerked away from the porthole and ran up the passage, through the lounge, along the deck, and through the saloon to the steps of the flying bridge. The hatch was open; she could see Jonathan's muscular brown legs, his white shorts. She climbed up until her head and shoulders were above the floor level.

"Where are we going?" She hated the tremor in her voice.

He looked down at her briefly and then back through the windshield. "Tell you later. At the moment, I've got to get through this mess."

She climbed the rest of the way up to the flying bridge and looked around. The waterway was crowded with boats. Big ones and little ones. Outboards, cruisers, sailboats. A lot of the little catamarans that the tourists rented. Charlie had spoken of them with infinite disgust one day. He had said that people who knew nothing about sailing rented them, and so you knew nothing about what they were going to do, because they didn't know themselves. And if you ran into them or they ran into you, it was still your fault because sailboats always have the right of way. She sat down in the other seat and waited. The canopy had been rolled back, and the sun was hot on her head, but the breeze was almost too cool. She pushed her hair out of her eyes and thought that the first thing she would do when she got back to Tarpon City was to get her hair cut. Sitting there, she realized that her anger had disappeared, leaving a dull, hopeless ache that was somehow worse than justifiable anger. She shivered and rubbed her arms to warm them, watching the big bow of *The Hideout* thread carefully through the teeming mass of other boats. Finally, Jonathan turned his attention to her.

"I'm taking you to another island," he said. "To a place where Lonigan won't find you."

"You could have simply sent me home with the crew," she said dully. "If I had left with Rolf, Rick would never connect me with you at all."

Jonathan's glance flickered over her face, which she knew was sulky and miserable. "I'm sorry," he said, his voice patient. "I was wrong. I shouldn't have asked you if you'd been in touch with Lonigan. Is that what you want to hear? An apology?"

It left a lot to be desired. But he *had* said he was

sorry. He had admitted he was wrong.

"It helps," she said. "But I think you know a lot more than you're telling me. Rick knew I was on this boat. He didn't just happen to see me; he was waiting. But he didn't know I was with you, or he wouldn't have thought Rolf was my—my lover."

Jonathan sighed. There was nothing but blue water in front of them now; they had left the bustling harbor behind. He sat back in his seat.

"Lonigan knew you were on this boat within a few hours of his arrival in Tarpon City," he said. "He knew the name of the boat, who owned it, and where it was headed."

"That's impossible. He couldn't have known any of that."

"It's not impossible, just crazy. He told Lance what happened, and Lance told me. Lonigan went to the newspaper office and found out where you lived. He went there first, hoping you hadn't left yet. He talked to Bert Andrews, your landlord. Andrews told him that an old fisherman had come by very upset, to say that he had seen your cat on the deck of a yacht named *The Hideout*, which was heading toward the ocean. He figured the people on the yacht had found the cat in the water, that you must have turned over your canoe. He had looked everywhere for you, and he wanted to organize a search. At last Andrews managed to convince the fisherman that it had to be some other Manx cat, because your canoe was stored and you were on vacation and had taken the cat with you." He stopped and grinned at her ruefully. "He was the fisherman we slowed down for on our way out of Fisherman's Cove, I suppose. He was close enough to get a good look at the cat on the bow, and to read the name of the boat. Anyway—and I find this amazing— on the strength of that unlikely story, Lonigan went to Customs to check the departure list. Naturally, he found what he was looking for."

"It's not amazing. Rick is very thorough—and he

gave me the cat." Lacey saw from Jonathan's expression that he didn't like what she had said, and added hastily, "So that's why he came to Nassau."

"No. He wasn't going to come here at first. He's been to the islands before. He knows how many small cays there are, and how impossible it is to find a boat that wants to stay hidden. He called, instead—Nassau, Freeport, West End—but we were still at the Lily banks, and no one he called knew anything about us. But when Lance called to find Marla, they both came over..." He gave her a somber, speculative glance. "Lance said Lonigan was hot to find the boat as soon as he arrived because he wanted to see you. So Lance told him there wasn't anyone on the boat but the crew. He said that you were the guest of one of the crewmen and that he didn't think a former lover would be welcome."

She stared straight ahead, her face reddening. "That wouldn't stop Rick," she said finally. "Not if he hadn't seen the situation for himself. He'd check it out, make sure you weren't aboard."

"I guess you're right," he said shortly, "since he did come down. But I don't think he was looking for me. Let's forget it."

"Not yet. I want to know how it went last night when you saw him—and Marla. Was Rick finally convinced that you do your own painting?"

"They weren't there," he said abruptly. "Don't worry about it. Lance is going to take care of everything." His big hands moved on the wheel, and the yacht made a long, sweeping curve. He pushed the throttle and gained speed. "Want to know where we're going?" He gave her a sudden, carefree grin. "Eleuthera. You'll like it. But right now, I'm hungry. How about making some sandwiches?"

It was obvious that he wasn't going to tell her anything more, she thought as she climbed down from the bridge. He trusted Lance; he didn't trust her. Somehow, she thought Lance had planned it that way. He was a devious man... so why did Jonathan trust him?

In the galley, she discovered that starvation wouldn't be a problem. The refrigerator was full, the small freezer loaded with steak, lobster, and shrimp. She found pastrami, rye bread and a small crock of horseradish-spiked mustard. She made two big sandwiches for Jonathan and a small one for herself. The coffee pot, secured in its gimbaled bracket, was still half-full, so she poured two mugs. She made two trips up with food, taking Jonathan's plate and cup first. When she sat down to eat, he was finishing his first sandwich.

"Maybe I won't miss Rolf at all," he said, glancing at her. "How are you on dinners? I remember you're an expert at breakfast."

"I can cook when I have to," she said, looking away from him, knowing he was referring to the breakfast she'd cooked that first morning in the old house, when he had forced her down on the leather couch.

"We'll eat out."

She laughed and finished her sandwich, then took the plates below. Washing them, she wondered about Eleuthera. She knew it wouldn't be as crowded as Nassau; there were no other cities of any size in the Bahamas. Suddenly, she wanted a place to stay on shore, a bed that didn't sway, an area to stroll without pushing through hordes of tourists. She needed to walk, to think. When she went back up to the bridge, she asked Jonathan if there were inns or cottages on Eleuthera.

"Tired of the boat, or the company?"

"I'd just like a change."

"You're in luck. That's exactly what I have in mind." He stood, stretching, his gaze sweeping the sea around them and coming back to the compass. He steadied the boat on course and reached to twist a dial, then punched a button below the console. "There. Now we'll stay on course. You're the lookout. Watch for anything floating, including boats. Yell if you see something we have to miss. I'm going down to call ahead for a berth."

His broad shoulders and tousled head disappeared down the hatch, and she stared at the wheel. It turned slowly to starboard and then slightly back to port, correcting for the southeast breeze. The autopilot really worked. She leaned on the frame of the windshield and narrowed her eyes against the glare of sun on water. A small dot on the horizon grew rapidly and became a freighter, pushing a white, foamy grin ahead of it. There was nothing else around them. New Providence and its bevy of attendant islets had dropped into the misty blue distance. This was open sea. For the first time since they had left the old house, she and Jonathan were alone, yet they had brought all their problems along. Rick's visit had made Jonathan angry and suspicious, and Lance Randall, somehow, was feeding the flames.

Below, Jonathan had evidently reached the person he wanted. She could hear his voice, warm and friendly, his deep laugh. Another trusted friend, she guessed, because he sounded as he did when he talked to Charlie. With others, his voice was always different, colder. Even with Lance, she realized suddenly. Even when he spoke of Lance. Maybe he didn't trust him as much as she thought he did. Yet some close tie bound them together...

The freighter was much closer now. It seemed to be on a course that would take it to their port side, but— She turned and went to look down the hatch.

"Jonathan?"

He interrupted his conversation. "I have to go," he said into the microphone. "We're on autopilot, and my woman is watching. She just called me. Okay, great. Good-bye."

She stepped away and went to lean on the frame again as he came up the steps. My woman, he had said. Well, she was his woman, undoubtedly one of a parade. Perhaps Madame Li had been only a little premature when she had taken her status for granted, viewing the assortment of clothes as a preliminary payment for value received. She frowned and looked away from him, waving a hand at the freighter.

"It seems to be planning to miss us," she said. "But it's close. And big."

"Right," he said and sat down, disengaging the autopilot and taking the wheel. "The wake would have rattled us around." He turned away from the path of the freighter until it passed, and then, as the subsiding waves of the wake approached, he turned into them to slide over gently. "We've got a berth at a little marina near the north end of the island," he said with satisfaction, "and we have a car to use. A friend in Governor's Harbour will open up the house." He grinned, the bronzed skin crinkling around his eyes. "We should be there in time for dinner. Wait until you see the beach."

"A house? Why not just a motel, or a cottage?"

"The house is much nicer, much more comfortable. Much more private." His glance was amused and intimate. "And there's a restaurant close by."

She looked away. "I think I'll go below," she said coolly. "I want to check up on Cabot."

Max slept unconcernedly under the blue awning at the stern, but Cabot, irritated, hugged the wall in an effort to avoid the fine spray blowing past. Lacey picked him up and took him with her to the lounge, put him down on the thick carpet, and watched him sit down in a patch of sunlight and begin to clean his soft gray fur with an expression of distaste.

"Too salty, I suppose," she said. "Well, we all have our problems." She went through to her cabin with its mirrored wall, examined the dark tufts of hair that framed her flushed face, ran her fingers through them, feeling the sticky dampness of salt. She stepped out of her clothes and went into the shower. Being well groomed just might restore her pride.

Chapter 11

LATER, DRESSED IN cream-colored slacks, a cool blouse of amber cotton, a matching turban over her freshly washed hair, she went back to the flying bridge and stood lookout again to give Jonathan a chance to stretch his cramped muscles and have another cup of coffee. This time there was no reason to alert him. A few small cruisers passed at a distance, and one slow-moving Chinese junk with all sails set, seemingly alive with tanned couples in bathing suits who waved at her enthusiastically as they drifted past. She gazed after them enviously. They were having a wonderful time—happy and free. But perhaps they thought the same of her, standing on the flying bridge of a luxurious yacht, heading for one of the Bahama islands.

"You're smiling," Jonathan accused, climbing back up to the bridge. "I thought you had recently established a no-smiling policy."

"Was I that bad?"

"Nearly." He hadn't taken his seat yet. There was nothing in sight now to avoid, and he stood beside her, studying her face. "Why have you been so solemn? Are you having second thoughts?"

Was he always going to know what she was thinking? "If I had any, they're gone," she said, consigning Madame Li and her cynicism to the nether regions. To be fair, she had flung herself into Jonathan's arms, knowing that it was only for a week, more or less. How could she blame him? It wasn't his fault that she wanted more, that she found herself dreaming of a future together. She smiled. "I'm looking forward to seeing a new island," she added, to change the subject. "Tell me about Eleuthera."

"I'll show it to you," he said. "Right now, you need to pack a bag. We'll be there in a little over an hour." He tipped up her chin and kissed her lightly. "No second thoughts, Lacey, not ever. Not about us. Now go below and look in the chest under the bench. You'll find a light bag. Put in a bathing suit—and forget the nightgowns."

Below, she rummaged in the storage box and found a nylon case like the ones Charlie and Rolf had carried. Jonathan seemed suddenly different, happier and more relaxed, she thought as she began to pack. Was he simply happy to be going to Eleuthera? Or was it that he felt things were going well, that his life wouldn't be changed, after all. He could still paint in solitude in the old house on Fisherman's Cove, and no one would know but Lance and Charlie and Rolf... but she would know.

Shutting the storage box, she took off her turban and brushed her hair until it shone. Then she picked up the carelessly packed nylon bag and left the cabin, standing for a moment at the foot of the companionway that led up to the saloon. Her life would be changed. She couldn't go back to *The Clarion,* to the apartment on the bay. Living there, she would know when Jonathan came back from New York again, and she wouldn't be able to stay away, not now. She would make an utter fool of herself, she realized helplessly. No. She would have to run again, as she had from Rick, but for a far different reason. Carrying the nylon case along the deck, she made her resolve. When it was over here, then it would be over for her, too.

"Still, he trusts Lance Randall more than I would," she said to Cabot as she passed him in the lounge. The cat blinked his yellow eyes at her and looked toward the door. Max was standing outside, peering in, his short tail flagging. Lacey let him in. He thanked her with a solid bump of his nose against her hip and went to flop thumpingly on the rug beside the cat.

Lacey smiled grimly. "Remember," she said to Cabot, "it's only a shipboard romance. These things never last." She felt the boat slow beneath her and begin to turn. There had been no land in sight. Curious, she left her bag in the saloon and climbed up to the flying bridge.

They were easing into what appeared to be a blue river bordered by the emerald-azure water over a reef. Ahead was a tree-fringed strand barely rising above the surface of the water. Beyond the strand she could see the outline of higher land, misty in the distance.

Jonathan was standing at the wheel now, peering closely at the water ahead. He gave her no more than a flick of a glance. "Tricky, here," he commented. "I'm following the blue..."

She watched, occasionally holding her breath. The blue of deeper water snaked through the reef; coral heads reared on either side to threaten the boat's smooth hull; small, brilliant fish fled from the boat's shadow as if from a monstrous shark. She grew so engrossed in watching that when she looked up again the island was startlingly close. The tall masts of sailboats stood clear against the sky, dwarfing the stunted mangroves along the shore. More land had appeared, running off into the northeast and out of sight. Overhead, a plane droned, ever louder as it dropped slowly toward the horizon before them. The blue river they traveled suddenly widened, and *The Hideout* picked up speed.

"How big is Eleuthera?"

"A hundred miles long," Jonathan said and added, grinning, "five miles wide. A crooked backbone sticking out of the ocean. But beautiful. We're near the northern end; the house is close to the middle." He sat back, relaxing. "The navigation is easy from here on in. The pink building you see behind those masts is the club. We'll leave the boat at the club marina and drive the car to the house. Are you packed?"

She nodded. "Except for putting Cabot in his travel

carrier and getting together a carton of food from the galley."

He laughed. "Neither is necessary. The cat will behave in the back seat with Max, and Eleuthera is the bread basket of the Bahamas. They grow everything here from cattle to pineapple. The food is one reason I love this island." He stood up, hunching fatigue from his shoulders, yawning. "Go below, mate, and be ready to toss a line."

On deck, she stood on the bow holding a line in nervous hands as they passed the moored sailboats, then entered a small basin where narrow docks spoked out to allow space for cruisers. A tall black man in khaki shorts and a brilliant red shirt stood on the end of one of the docks and waved a long arm. *The Hideout* turned toward him, coasted along the dock, and reversed, sliding so close that Lacey simply handed the line to the man, went aft, and looped the stern line around a cleat on the dock.

"Easy," she said as Jonathan joined her on deck. "Nothing to it. I'll hire on with you as a deckhand." Sudden happiness bubbled into laughter at his expression. "And I'll cook, too, if you insist."

"I'll never insist. I like the other choice better," he said, and turned to greet the tall man who had leaped to the deck and was coming toward them grinning.

"Wictah Kahh, miss," he said to Lacey, and enclosed her hand briefly in a strong, bony clasp. "'Ope you henjoys the stay." He clapped Jonathan on the shoulder with easy familiarity. "Bags to lift off, mon?"

In minutes, they were on the dock, Lacey following the men toward a parking lot with Cabot in her arms and Max beside her. They stowed bags in the trunk of a small car, the cat willingly went into the back seat with Max, and they drove off amid a flurry of good wishes for a pleasant 'oliday. Amused and bewildered, Lacey turned to Jonathan.

"What did he say his name was?"

"Victor Kerr. Don't you understand English? He's a fixture here—official greeter, I think. He's from Hopetown, in Abaco—or as he would say 'Opetown, in Habaco. Hopetown is where they mix up their aitches, their vees, and their double-u's." He laughed. "But he's handy to know when you need a berth or a car. And he's a good friend." He watched her laugh, and added warmly, "I think you 'ave decided to 'ave a pleasant 'oliday, miss. Am I right?"

She met his gaze, feeling the familiar jolt, a charged current of attraction. "Yes. It's great to be away from Nassau. There was a lot of tension there. Does anyone know where we are?"

"Lance will know when he sees we've left the dock. He knew I was thinking of leaving, and he'll guess that I've come to Eleuthera. But that's all right; I'm supposed to call him tomorrow, anyway."

"Why?" Mention of Lance Randall made her uncomfortable.

"I have to push him a bit. I'm afraid he needs it." For a moment, his voice was hard, and then he reached for her hand, holding it gently, caressing her wrist with his thumb. "Don't worry about Lance. I can handle him. Lonigan was the one who had me worried—and it seems you took care of him." His hand tightened. "You and Max." He laughed. "My dog! I hope you never set him against me."

"I hope you never give me reason," she said, her voice deceptively gentle, and laughed at his startled glance. "I would hate to see Max torn between two loyalties."

He was silent, driving along an uninspired stretch of shell road that meandered between clumps of stunted island growth and seemed to go nowhere in particular.

"Has that happened to *you*, Lacey?" he asked finally. "I've wondered. You're a—well, call it a member of the media. You have a friend, Richard Lonigan, who is trailing a story he thinks is important. You used to help him do that." His gaze swept her face. "Have you felt divided in your loyalties?"

She turned toward him in the seat, tucking her feet up under her. "Let's get this straight, once and for all," she said. "Rick gave me my first job—and at first I was pretty thrilled to be working for an internationally known columnist. But I learned fast. Rick could have made a fine newspaperman, except that he's got an ugly urge to go for the jugular when the news concerns a celebrity, and he doesn't care how much harm he does. He never makes anything up, and he never tells a direct lie, but he sifts through facts and puts the ones he wants together. It's worse than lying, because it's impossible to fight. He hurts people on purpose. He's rotten. I don't owe him any loyalty. You couldn't even explain the word to him."

Jonathan stared at the road, his face still. "But you must have cared for him. You lived with him."

"Yes," she said flatly, "I did care for him once. That makes a difference to you." It wasn't a question, it was a statement of fact. She watched his hands tighten on the steering wheel.

"It might," he said, "If..." His eyes narrowed as he glanced at her. "Why did you leave him?"

"I think I just told you," she said, her voice dangerously soft, "didn't I? Why would I want to stay with him after I found out what he was like? We fought continually until I realized that I couldn't stop him from doing what he was doing. He likes it—hurting people. By the time I left, we were bitter enemies."

"Lonigan told Lance you ran away because you were jealous of another woman. He said you were wrong, that there wasn't anyone else for him. He said he was still crazy about you—and was going to get you back."

Lacey thrust her feet to the floor and sat up. "That," she said, "is a lie. Lance's lie. Rick wouldn't have said it. What is Lance trying to do?" Unexpected fury shook her. "Lance has racked up quite a number of lies now, hasn't he? He's had you helping to set up some of them. That studio near Gambier. You helped with that—and it won't put Rick off. He'll still look for the artist who really paints for Jonathan Grey... until he is absolutely sure that there is no such person." She stopped, breathing deeply. "I guess I understand why you helped with the Gambier studio—to hide the fact of the old house. But I hate it—the pretense, the falseness..."

His face was pale, his eyes fixed on the road. "The old house isn't all I've been hiding," he said slowly. "I keep wondering what you'll think when you find out the rest."

"Tell me and you'll know," she said, startled into curiosity.

He laughed. "I wish I could. I'd get a frank opinion, wouldn't I?" His arm went around her, pulled her close, holding her for a moment. "You're a featherweight, but you're a real tough fighter, aren't you?" His eyes were gleaming with amusement and something like relief. "Let's stop this. We're supposed to be having fun."

"Let's," she said. Her fury had blown itself out. The touch of his arm, the hug, had warmed her. She turned to look out again and discovered that the road now ran east along a shore where calm aquamarine water was dotted by long-legged, graceful birds and large, pale rocks that rose above the surface, each with its own tiny beach of sand. They were coming to a settlement of small houses and a few stores. Behind the settlement, a plane rose lazily into the blue and passed over them at an angle to the west. Lacey looked with interest at the pinkish roads of the little town, at the natives going in and out of the stores.

"Fishermen," she said. "I saw them on the Nassau quays in those odd straw hats and dungarees. They dress differently from the others."

"Divers from Spanish Wells," he said. "They fish with nets, and dive beside them to keep the sharks away from their fish. Not the safest way to make a living. Want to go diving on a reef?"

Lacey shuddered. "Not with sharks."

Jonathan grinned. "I wish we had a month. I'd like to show you Harbour Island and Spanish Wells. And Gregory Town—you'd like that. We'll catch a glimpse as we pass. It's like a village in Cornwall." He glanced at her, his blue eyes warm. "We'll do it all next time."

She considered that in silence. He probably meant it, right now. But once this interlude was over, he would be heading for New York with his paintings. Marla would help him to forget her, to reimmerse himself in the art world. That was his world, and Marla was exactly right for that world. Lacey sighed, looking out.

The road was hooking around a narrow neck of land between the ocean and the enclosed bay on the west. It was midafternoon, and heat blew in until they rolled up the car windows and turned on the air conditioner. The scenery was now varied with cliffs, and the coastal village of Gregory Town did have an English flavor. Lacey saw stocky cattle, hock-deep in rich grass, and everywhere were fields of vegetables, green and healthy plants that made her hungry to look at them.

"Why so quiet?"

"My eyes are busy," she answered. It was impossible to keep from smiling at him. He seemed so oversized in the little car, his long legs folded up, his hands too big for the wheel, his shoulders too wide for the small seat. It took something as big as *The Hideout* to put him in proportion. But he looked relaxed and amazingly pleased. "You like it here, don't you?"

"My island," he said, sounding as if he owned it all. "Everyone who spends time in the Bahamas has a favorite. This one's mine." His glance at her was almost possessive. "You'll feel the same way. Eleuthera is nothing like Nassau."

"Have you been to all the islands?"

He laughed. "Not yet. There are twenty-nine of them. And over six hundred cays. There's a lot left to explore..."

She thought of him wandering the cobalt and turquoise sea in his boat, searching for new places, more beauty to put into his paintings. He would enjoy the unique flavor of every one, free to stay or go. She tried to imagine him in New York and failed.

"Where do you live in New York?"

He glanced at her, smiling faintly. "I'm never quite sure I'm living, in New York. Not after this..." He slowed the car, looking off to the side. "This is, I suppose, what you would call the outskirts of Governor's Harbour."

A steep hill stretched up before them. On either side of the road were homes built in old New England styles. He drove faster again, smiling.

"It won't be long now. Through the town and then halfway down the ridge."

She sat forward, feeling a flutter of excited anticipation, which seemed rather childish but enjoyable. The car climbed into a village drowsing in sunlight, people strolling, narrow streets with little traffic. The austere style of New England buildings seemed out of place in a tropical setting, and the new modern structures looked even more alien. There was a bank, an Anglican church, shops, and a supermarket.

"Should we buy food?"

He shook his head. "There will be food at the house. Victor's friend will have stocked the refrigerator."

The road dropped off past the town, leading southeast again. She was silent, waiting with a strange, excited feeling of presentiment, of being led into something that would be a landmark in her life—whether for good or ill she could not know. When the car turned off on a shell-surfaced lane, the feeling grew stronger, and she held her breath as they traveled east through a stand of thin pines and burgeoning tropical undergrowth. Through the slender trunks of the trees, she could see a dark red roof; when she looked back along the twisting lane she saw that the main road was now out of sight. Then the rolling land dipped and the undergrowth cleared out, leaving a straight view to the house—a soft-toned building that blended into the landscape, the lower wall faced with coral slabs, the rest of it weathered pine planks the same shade as Cabot's pale gray fur. Beyond it, a glimpse of blue, the white curl of waves. In the back seat, Max whimpered with eagerness.

"It's perfect." She was leaning forward, as eager as Max. "How did you ever find it?"

He skirted a bougainvillaea vine that dripped flower-laden branches over the lane, and drove into a parking space behind the house. "I didn't exactly find it. I had it built. It's mine." His eyes were questioning, vulnerable. "Do you like it?"

"Anyone would," she said with conviction, and scrambled from the car, seeing that the lower part of the building behind the coral slabs was a cavernous garage, a dim space of huge pillars that held the living space some fifteen feet above the ground. "What a view of the ocean you must have from up there," she said, turning back to him, trying to hold down her excitement as she saw his amused expression.

"Yes. But that's not the reason for the elevation," he said, opening the back door of the wagon. Max dashed out, a black and rust blur, and disappeared under the house. "The height makes the house safer during hurricanes, when the ocean arrives with water and sand to scrub out the garage." Cabot had come warily to the open car door to inspect the ground, and Max came tearing back from underneath the house to place a red rubber ball at Jonathan's feet, his tail beating the air. Lacey laughed and went to the car, picking Cabot up and hugging him.

"I'm glad you brought me here," she said. "This is what people dream of when they dream of islands." She stopped, surprised at her own words and somewhat embarrassed. "I don't care," she said to his grin. "It's true. And I'll always have this to remember..." She put Cabot down and whirled, running lightly away from Jonathan, around the house.

"I've got to see the beach," her call came floating back to him. "It's part of the dream..."

Chapter 12

"THE SAND IS PINK!" She swung toward him as he came down the beach, her face lit by the slanting afternoon sun, her sandals dangling from one hand, the bottoms of her slacks wet from the waves that swirled and foamed around her bare feet. "Pink, and as soft as powder." She looked down, wriggling her toes deeper, ignoring the water that swirled up again. "How did you ever manage that?"

"One of the basic luxuries," he said. "It comes with the property. Don't you want to see the inside of the house? Especially the kitchen? I'm starved."

She gave an exaggerated sigh and, pulling her feet from the holes she had made, came to him. Clinging to his arm, leaning against him, she raised a foot to brush ineffectually at the glistening coat of sand.

"A new universal law," she said. "When a dream comes true, it must be crushed immediately by grim reality. Yes, I'll look at the kitchen. And cook, too, before you ask. Are you always hungry?"

"Yes...always." He bent and swept her up in his arms as he had the first day they met, holding her tight against his chest and walking quickly toward the house. "In fact, I often feel like a boy with his nose pressed against a candy-store window." He laughed, looking down at her flushed face, and mounted the coral slab steps that led to a balcony porch at the front of the house. He kept an arm around her as he set her on her feet and unlocked the front door.

"I took the bags in through the back," he said, "and put them in our bedroom. It's on the left—to catch the southeast breeze. I think you'll like it." He paused. "There's another bedroom, but it's haunted."

"By what?"

"A ghost, what else? A ravenous male ghost, who will stamp in during the middle of the night and wake you by crawling into your bed. Then he—"

"Stop there," she said quickly. "I'm terrified. I'll stay with you."

"I thought you might," he said, and pushed open the door.

She stepped into a long, high-ceilinged room that took up half the house. That it was a man's home was evident. Masculine, with a color scheme of earthy shades of browns and golds. She stood on decorative straw matting that served as a rug, and looked at heavy wood furniture upholstered in rough homespun, driftwood tables that held brass lamps with cream shades. The walls were cream with dark woodwork; dark beams crossed the light ceiling. There were books and a collection of shells in a tall bookcase. It would have been a plain room, almost too simple, if it hadn't been for the painting that dominated the west wall. It was huge, framed in heavy wood, and its colors, even in the pale evening light, gave a glowing warmth to the room. She went forward to stand before it, hypnotized by its beauty and by her own memory.

It was the old house on the mangrove-shaded island. Not a line had been changed. There was the bare window of his bedroom where she had stood to watch the path. The crooked steps led to the sagging porch. Around it, the mangrove trees pressed close, their branches of glistening dark green reached to shield the old, bleached wood, just as she remembered. But it didn't look the same. It reached out, with warmth and welcome. There was something—something that said this is home, you are safe here... something that made you want to run up the path and through the door. She swung around. "You painted your grandfather inside his house," she said. "I can't see him, but I know he's there."

Jolted, he came toward her slowly, his eyes flickering from the painting to her face. "What do you know about my grandfather?" His gaze was curiously defensive, as if she had breached some inner wall, had discovered a secret.

"Pike Farrell knew him. And Pike is a garrulous old man with a gift for communicating his thoughts. He admired your grandfather very much." She turned back to the painting. "But Pike didn't tell me you were so close to your grandfather when you were young. It's just that I see—here—the way you felt about him."

His hands clasped her shoulders and turned her around. "You're dangerous," he said, only half-smiling. "You see too much." Roughly, he pulled her into the circle of his arms. "What if I painted the house with you in it? What would you see then?"

Love, she thought. But she had secrets to defend, too. "I suppose," she said lightly. "I might see bars on the windows..."

"Not necessary," he said, after a moment of silence. "I could paint Max outside, ferociously on guard. Now, may I introduce you to the kitchen?"

The archway to the kitchen was behind an intricately carved wooden screen at the end of the long west wall. She followed him around the screen and found a narrow room with the usual collection of cabinets, a big refrigerator, and a modern stove and sink. Everything ranged along the walls, making a corridor that led to the north end of the room, which was all glass, a huge picture window that looked out along the pink beach. A driftwood dining table had been placed there, with cane-seated ladder-back chairs. Everything shone, neat and orderly. The refrigerator hummed efficiently; the stove top gleamed with recent polishing.

"Ready for action," Jonathan said, and opened the refrigerator to peer in. "Ah. Steak. Olivia never forgets my favorite foods."

At the sink, washing her hands, Lacey thought how much he looked like any other male at an open refrigerator. Inquisitive and hopeful.

"Olivia?" she inquired.

"Victor's friend. She's guardian of the house when I'm not here." He rummaged in the refrigerator, bringing out the package of steak, a head of lettuce, tomatoes, scallions. Hands full, he kneed the door shut and plopped his burdens on the wooden counter. "You make a salad; I'll broil the steaks. There's a bottle of wine in the refrigerator. Olivia left a bowl of fresh-cut pineapple, and there's cheese to go with it. Coffee in the cabinet, brandy if you like..." He stopped, looking at her. "All right?"

"Just right," she said, meaning it. It all seemed part of the dream, like the pink sand, the secluded island house, the warm breeze from the ocean. A chapter added to the memory she was to have, later. She found a wooden bowl and started the salad. As an afterthought, she dismissed the word "later." There was no later in dreams, as there was no past. Only the present...

They ate at the driftwood table, watching the twilight deepen on the beach, the sand pass from pink to dusky rose, the blue water darken to indigo. As they finished their dinner, she knew he watched her more than he did the scene outside, for she was sensitive now to his gaze. It seemed to warm her where it touched, moving from her face to her hands, traveling over her neck and shoulders, her breasts, outlined by the thin cotton blouse. When she glanced at him, his eyes darkened like the ocean outside; the smile on his broad mouth was intimate, sensual. She got up quickly and began to clear the table, feeling the throbbing of her blood, a pulsing warmth that ran through her like wine.

"Dishes," she said, in what she hoped was a normal, disparaging tone, for somehow he had made her feel shy.

"At least, there aren't too many..." She went back and forth briskly, putting things away, washing the dishes energetically. He got up and found a dish towel, came to stand beside her and dry the dishes awkwardly as she put them in a drainer.

"I'm only a learner," he said as a dish slipped from his grasp. "Domestic scenes aren't my specialty."

"Nor mine," she said. "I keep wondering how I got involved in this."

"As I remember," he said meditatively, "it began when you stepped on an oyster. Which reminds me that the shells on my beach are not that sharp. Have you ever been swimming at night?"

For a moment, she didn't answer. Her imagination had leaped ahead, giving her a clear mental picture of the two of them swimming together in the dark, warm water. She took the dish cloth from him and hung it up carefully. "I've swum at night," she said. "There was a pool at the Y when I was a teenager. It was very nice." She turned, sliding her arms around his neck. "But we had to wear bathing suits. Do we have to wear bathing suits here?"

His mouth twitched. "Of course not. I think there's a local law against it. I'm sure I've seen the signs saying bathing suits may be worn during daylight hours only. And even though this is a private beach, I think we should obey the law, don't you?"

She kissed him, sighing, thinking how it would be...

It was very dark, but clear, with bright stars in a cloudless sky. Lacey could see the glimmer of foam on small waves, the dark water swirling on the sand. Jonathan had brought a blanket and beach towels, and he spread the blanket on dry sand, disrobing quickly, dropping his shirt and shorts on the blanket.

"Let me help you," he said, reaching for her. "You wear too many clothes."

She laughed, evading his hands. "I came here to swim," she said, kicking off her shoes. His intentions were very clear. She took off her shirt, the cool night air on her bare skin a shock of pleasure. Stepping out of her slacks, she felt his arms slide around her to unhook her bra, his hands enclosing her freed breasts. She twisted in his arms and the hands dropped, pushing the lacy briefs from her hips, grasping rounded buttocks, urging her toward him. Her body responded instantly, swaying involuntarily against his. She put her hands flat on his warm chest. "Swim," she murmured, "remember?"

"Only vaguely," he said, laughing softly, "but maybe the water is cool enough to help." He turned, taking her hand. "Let's find out."

They ran toward the dark sea, plunging through the shallows, pushing on into deeper water, floundering, and then falling with tremendous splashes.

"Wild," Lacey gasped, coming up in chest-deep water. "How free it feels! Naked in the world..."

He laughed, shaking the water from his hair and eyes. "It will spoil you," he said, amused. "You'll learn to hate bathing suits." He lay back, his body rising, floating lazily. Half-submerged, his body gleamed wetly in the dim light, the great arch of his chest, the muscular thighs and arms, his strong profile turned to the starry sky. The water, she noted, had not been cool enough.

She moved toward him, her feet barely touching the sandy bottom in the buoyant water, feeling weightless and supple and completely natural, like Eve in a pool in Eden. She touched him with feather-light fingertips, trailing from knee to chest and back again, feeling him quiver beneath her touch.

"Careful," he warned, making his voice gruff. "If you excite me I'll sink."

"No, you won't," she promised softly. "I'll hold you up." She put her arms under his floating body and drew him close, his taut side against her breasts. "See? I can hold you." She leaned to nuzzle his flat belly, tonguing the tight navel, and went down with him as he lunged to grab her and sank. She came up in his arms, gasping again. "You'll drown me!"

"Only turn you into a mermaid," he said huskily, "to

torment lonely sailors." He was holding her tightly, her breasts crushed against his chest, his legs locked around hers. "Lacey..."

"Yes..." Welded against him, she had begun to flame. "Darling...oh, how you make me feel..."

"Tell me how I make you feel." He was staring down at the dim outlines of her face, her parted lips.

"Soft and warm...like fireworks...like Christmas morning," she whispered slowly. "Like part of you...and wanting the rest."

"That's what you are," he said, "all of those things." He kissed her, hard and demanding, his bulging arousal tight against her belly. "What are we doing out here, anyway?"

She smiled into the dark face so close to hers. "Waiting," she said caressingly, "waiting to make love again."

He eased his grip on her legs and lifted her, his feet settling firmly on the bottom. "Part of it we don't have to wait for," he said thickly. "Put your legs around me."

She gasped as he eased her down, cradling her hips against him, entering her strongly. They rocked, water-slick bodies sliding together in an increasingly sensual movement. In moments, she was alive with deep, hot pleasure; she moaned, making husky, incoherent sounds. She tightened her legs around him, leaned forward and kissed him, tangling her fingers in his wet hair. "Magic," she breathed. "You're magic." She teased his broad mouth with her tongue, tasting sharp salt and then the hot, tantalizing flavor of his open mouth as he arched into her in shuddering release. Her body answered his, squeezing down on him ecstatically, again and again. Then she could only lean against him and let the fire slowly cool.

They went back to the house late, wrapped in towels, their clothes bundled into the blanket beneath Jonathan's arm. Showering together, they still felt a sleepy desire. In the bedroom, where wind from the sea billowed the curtains over them, their lovemaking took on the slow cadence of the ocean, rising and falling, with a tide of passion that built to a steep wave, to peak and crash and spread through them like foam on the beach, receding slowly. Jonathan fell asleep with his arms still around her, but Lacey lay watching the curtains waft into the room, ballooning and falling in the wind.

In the middle of their lovemaking, he had called her his love—"My love, my dearest love." Words suited to the moment. How wonderful if he said them at other times, if he meant them. She pulled away carefully and turned over to face the other way, letting the breeze cool her heated skin. This would all be beautiful in memory, but parting was going to hurt like hell.

She woke early, too early. In the patch of sky outside the window, she could see that the stars were still there, though they were paling against a lighter blue. She lay still, breathing in the scent of the beach, and finally slipped out of bed, glancing back cautiously at Jonathan, who was still sleeping soundly, relaxed and sprawling over most of the bed. She was quiet, taking the first thing she found to wear—the two scraps of black satiny bikini—and dressing in the bathroom.

Sitting on the steps outside, she watched the day begin, the sun scattering gold on the pink sand, the small birds running along the shore, the clear turquoise waves lifting and rushing forward to spread white lace along the sand. A beauty as exquisite as passion, and as soon over.

The air warmed, and the beckoning of the waves became irresistible. She rose and went down the steps, the fresh breeze tossing her hair. Halfway down the sloping shore a sudden, careless joy sent her running. She plunged into a rising swell of glassy turquoise and came up like a seal, with her black hair streaming flat and shining. She played, discovering that the gentle current carried her toward the beach and a bit northward. It was safe, then, and when she tired she turned on her back and floated blissfully. Motionless, she put all thoughts of the future out of her mind. The sun on her body was warm and sensuous.

Then Jonathan was calling her, his voice hoarse. She opened her eyes and stood upright, her feet bumping the sandy bottom. The current had carried her far along the beach, but she could see the top of the house and Jonathan, striding toward her. She ran, splashing up on to dry sand; he stopped and then came toward her slowly. She saw with surprise that he was wearing slacks and a shirt.

"Sorry," she said, breathless. "I wasn't watching. I guess the current..." Her voice trailed away at the look on his pale face.

"You're lucky," he said shortly, "that you weren't swept out. That's not a swimming pool. Keep your eyes open." His eyes flicked over her, and he frowned. "You've had enough sun. In between those two strips of black satin, you're burned."

Subdued, she looked down and discovered he was right. "It's been hardly any time at all," she protested.

"In this latitude, it doesn't take much time." He turned away. "You'd better go inside. I'm on my way to Governor's Harbour to make that telephone call." He left her, his long legs taking him up the beach quickly to disappear around the house without a backward glance.

Slowly, she climbed the steps and sat down to brush the sand from her feet. He had sounded like an irate father, not a lover. He had been angry. Too angry to take her along, and she would have loved to go. She stood up, glancing along the beach to the spot where she had ended her blissful floating. At that distance, it would have been hard for Jonathan to see her in the water, impossible for him to know if she was breathing. Maybe it hadn't been anger that had made him pale and critical. Perhaps it had been worry. Fear. But didn't he know she could take care of herself?

Later, dressed in shorts and a knitted top, she went

for a walk with Max, leaving Cabot yawning disgustedly under the house. She walked farther than she had intended, lured on by the broken pieces of coral, the perfect small shells. Coming back, her pockets bulging with treasures and Max panting at her side, she saw chrome shining behind the house and hurried up the steps, hoping Jonathan wouldn't be angry again.

Lance Randall, his handsome face a study in surprise, wheeled to stare at her as she opened the door.

"So, you're here. Where's Jon? I supposed I would have to wait for both of you..."

Lacey stared at him, surprised and unsure, and then went to empty her pockets into a large wooden bowl on a table, thinking. "He should be here any minute," she said stiffly. "He went into town to make a telephone call." She raised her head and looked at Lance directly. "I thought the call was to you."

He laughed. "It probably was. But I wanted to speak to him in person." His eyes were making their usual calculations, roving over her. "I'm surprised you didn't go with him."

She ignored that, moving toward the kitchen. "Can I get you something to drink? Iced tea? A Coke?"

His eyes were narrowing, thoughtful as he stared at her. "A beer," he said absently, "if you have one."

She nodded, remembering that she had seen beer in the refrigerator. She left him with relief and went into the kitchen, pouring iced tea for herself and taking a bottle of beer and a mug for Lance. She peered hopefully down at the parking place and toward the winding lane. No sign yet of the small car. In the living room, Lance came to meet her, to take the bottle and mug from her hand. He was smiling, his eyes lazily good-humored, looking into hers.

"Actually," he said, going back to his chair, "I'm glad I found you alone. There is something rather important that I'd like to discuss with you, since we have the chance." He sat down, placing the mug on a table beside the chair, pouring the beer carefully. His brows were drawn together over his classically modeled nose as if he were thinking deeply, and Lacey found herself suddenly wary, wondering what new lie he was composing. But when he looked back at her, his face seemed open and friendly.

"We should get along well," he said. "We've got something in common. If I'm not mistaken, you're fond of Jon. And I'm one of his oldest and best friends."

She gave him a noncommittal smile and sat down on the couch. "And I'm one of his newest friends. I suspect that Jonathan has a good many friends besides us." She sipped her iced tea, wondering at his suddenly sharp eyes.

"Is that what you call him? Jonathan?"

"Why not? I know everyone else shortens it to Jon, but I like the full name better. He doesn't object." She looked at Lance defensively, and he smiled.

"No, of course he wouldn't—coming from you. But it's... unusual for him to use it."

He sat staring at the mug in his hand, and Lacey thought suddenly that she knew why he was surprised. He thought Jonathan had hidden his identity from her, as he did with everyone else in Florida. Lance didn't know she had guessed the name herself, from the painting in the old house. So, she thought, Jonathan didn't confide fully in Lance, after all. She was silent, waiting for him to speak again.

"Rick Lonigan tells me that you're a reporter—one of the best. Funny Jon didn't mention that, when we met at the Lily banks." Lance shifted his elegant body to a lounging position, smiling again, watching her through half-closed eyes.

She had heard the challenge in his voice. "Perhaps," she said evenly, "it didn't seem important to him. He isn't particularly interested in the media."

"Isn't he?" Lance drank, and set the mug down. "He should be. Publicity sells paintings." He rose from the chair, reaching into a pocket. "Good publicity, that is.

Not this kind..." He came closer to her and dropped a scrap of folded newspaper in her lap. "It was unwise of you to hurt Rick's pride by setting Max on him."

Her heart sank in a premonition of disaster. She picked up the clipping gingerly, her hands trembling as she unfolded it. Rick would be wiring in his copy while he was in the Bahamas, and it would be singularly appropriate if he used stories about people in the islands. Sure enough, the article Lance had given her was Rick's column. She saw the headline: "VIPs and Quips," with Rick's byline below it. The lead sentence told her that her premonition had been correct:

> Artist Jonathan Grey's talent for illusion may fail him when he tries to placate his true love, Marla Pomeroy, who has been languishing in Nassau while Grey's yacht, *The Hideout*, lives up to its name. The luxurious floating home is circling to other islands with a lady aboard who is allegedly Grey's latest playmate, Lacey Thomas. Grey insists that Lacey is the beloved of one of his crew, but his frequent absences from Marla's side seem to prove otherwise. Especially when one hears that *The Hideout* has moved on, which makes the chance of discovery small. Remember Lacey? You should, if you've been reading these pages long. She was a member of this column's research staff, before she faded into obscurity and became a small-town newspaper reporter. Lacey is a lovely bit of femininity, but perhaps not worth losing the equally lovely, influential Marla, whose father owns the Pomeroy Gallery, where Grey's paintings are exhibited...

Lacey stared at the clipping, pretending to read long after she had finished it. She wanted to cry, to scream, to tear the column to bits. Pride prevented her, and when she raised her eyes she seemed calm.

"Rick's as rotten as ever," she said. "It's hard to believe he would go so far, isn't it?" She folded the clipping neatly. It wasn't really hard for her to believe Rick would go so far. What was hard to believe was Jonathan's constant lying. When he had said he was meeting Lance, he was really "placating" Marla. And he had been with Rick, too. Rick never attributed statements to people unless he'd heard the words himself. So the times Jonathan had said he had avoided Rick and Marla, he had actually been with them. Had he ever told Lacey the truth? She was suddenly conscious that Lance was talking, had apparently been talking for some time.

"... And it couldn't have happened at a worse time, with the award ceremony scheduled at the gallery," he was saying. He was pacing nervously, his face alert, as if he were looking or listening for more trouble to arrive. "I hate to say this, Lacey, but if you are really fond of Jon, I think the best thing you could do is to put yourself out of the picture—now. When gossip gets ugly enough, it can hurt a career."

She wanted to say that a career was not all that could be hurt, but she only nodded. "I'm sure you're right; it's the best thing to do. I'll leave as soon as I can."

"I'll help you," he said quickly. "If you want, I can have you out of here—out of the islands—in an hour. All you have to do is pack your clothes. I'll drive you to the airport on the other side of Governor's Harbour—it's just minutes away."

"I'll have to explain to Jonathan first."

Lance gave a short laugh. "I suppose it's natural to want to do that. But forgive me if I point out that your explanation might not please him. He's going to be very embarrassed, isn't he? I mean, it's one thing for him to play around a bit before he ties the final knot with Marla—and I'm sure you enjoyed it, too—but it's no fun for him to get caught at it."

Lacey closed her eyes, trying to visualize Jonathan's face as she showed him the clipping, when he found out she knew—and that Marla knew, too, now. What would he say? Would he get angry and say it was all lies? Or would he try to laugh it off? She got up suddenly, letting the paper fall to the floor.

"I'll go now," she told Lance tersely. "It won't take me long to pack."

Chapter 13

LANCE WAS HURRYING her down the back steps, her bag in his hand, when Jonathan drove in through the winding lane. He honked the horn at them, then stopped the car and got out, his smile fading as he saw the bag in Lance's hand.

"Well," he said, advancing, "where are you taking my girl, Lance?"

Smoothly, Lance handed Lacey her bag. "I'll talk to him," he said, his voice low. "Go back inside and wait."

She hesitated, but he pushed the handle of the bag into her hand. "It will be better, coming from me," he insisted. "Not as embarrassing. Go!"

She retreated first to the kitchen; then, when she heard them coming up the back steps together, she fled to the bedroom. She flung the bag on the bed and sat down, her throat thick and hurting. She decided that she didn't want to see Jonathan at all after he realized what had happened, and knew that she knew...

The two men were in the kitchen, talking. She could hear Lance's high-pitched voice, sounding injured and plaintive. "Good Lord, Jon, if I had known you would resent my presence here so much, I wouldn't have come. After all, I was only trying to help. Lacey wants to leave—to go home..."

She listened tensely for Jonathan's reply. It wasn't as easy to make out what he was saying; his voice was deep and rumbling dangerously. "I told you what to do. I've given you every chance to do it—more time than you needed. And I told you I'd call. You knew I wanted to be here alone. That should have been sufficient. Dammit, it *is* sufficient! Give Marla my message, and if necessary, tell Lonigan, too. They'll tell the world, won't they?"

"But you don't realize how hard a job that is. I need more time... Marla isn't going to take this well."

The rumble of Jonathan's voice was even deeper now, and Lacey strained her ears in vain for his words. She thought how angry he sounded, how authoritative. Whatever was going on between the two of them, it was obvious that Jonathan was in control and that Lance had disobeyed an order. From what she'd heard, it sounded as if there was much more to the problem than Rick's column. She turned and flung herself full length on the bed, wishing wholeheartedly that she and Lance had escaped before Jonathan returned. How could she even walk past him on her way to Lance's car without showing how she felt? She willed her anger to mount, to grow high enough to burn out the pain.

She heard their voices once more, from the parking space below. She leaped up and went to the window, looking down from behind the curtains. Her heart sank farther as she realized Lance was leaving without her; he had not been able to convince Jonathan that it would be better for her to leave now. The two men were standing by Lance's car, and Lance was talking rapidly, his expressive hands gesturing. He looked again as he had on the boat at the Lily banks, as if he were trying to ingratiate himself with Jonathan, to convince him that everything was going well. His smile, though bright, was strained. Jonathan's back was tense, his shoulders bunched. Then he stepped back, relaxing, nodding. He turned to face the house, but Lacey kept her eyes on Lance as he got into the car. As she watched, his smile faded; his handsome profile was petulant as he drove away, the tires of his car spurting shell as he turned down the winding lane and disappeared.

She left the window and went into the big room,

hearing Jonathan in the kitchen, opening the refrigerator door. She continued walking, going outside to stand on the balcony and look out over the ocean. The wind had come up; it blew the hair back from her face and flattened her clothes against her body. Offshore, two large sailboats were heeled over and running before the breeze, as graceful as enormous white birds, She thought of the people on board, happy and engrossed in handling the boats, sitting in the sun and wind, laughing. She wished she were with them—or anywhere but here.

The door opened behind her, and she tensed but did not turn around.

"Would you mind telling me why you asked Lance to take you to the airport?"

His voice told her one thing; he was not going to laugh it off.

"It was his suggestion," she said tightly, "but I approved. He didn't want you to be embarrassed."

A hand caught her arm, swung her around. Jonathan's eyes had darkened to indigo with anger. "Embarrassed about what?"

She jerked her arm away. "Oh, come on," she said, disgusted. "Lance must have told you about Rick's column. The column," she added in sudden, high anger, "that proves what a liar you are."

Blood rushed beneath his tan, turning his skin rich and dark. "What are you talking about, Lacey? Watch what you say to me..." He turned away, fighting for control. When he turned back, his voice was quiet. "All Lance told me was that you felt our 'affair' had lasted quite long enough, that it was time for you to bow out. He said he supposed you were simply tired of it, and that I probably was, too." His eyes rested on her, coldly questioning. "Frankly, I didn't believe him. I think you must have another reason."

"I do," she said, calmer. "Lance was just too cowardly to tell you. Wait, I'll get the article." She went past him into the big room, looking for the clipping. It wasn't on

Kisses Incognito

the floor by the couch, where it had fallen when she stood up. She looked on the tables. Undoubtedly Lance had picked it up, but where had he put it? She went into the kitchen and checked the wastebasket, which was empty. She went back out on the balcony and faced Jonathan.

"Either he took Rick's column with him, or he gave it to you. Which?"

He looked at her levelly. "If there is such a thing as a clipping from Lonigan's column, I don't have it."

It was her turn to fight for control. Tears of anger and frustration stood in her eyes. "Lance must have taken it with him," she said, "but I don't really need the clipping. I remember it word for word. I doubt I will ever forget it."

He sat down. "Take your time reciting it," he said. "I wouldn't want to miss anything."

Her anger flared at his disbelief, his sarcasm, and somehow it strengthened her. "You realize you're the last to hear it," she said. "All of North America has read it by now. It was the lead item in the column and began with your name..." Standing before him, she repeated Rick's glib phrasing in the flat tone of a child reciting poetry in class, faltering halfway through when his eyes went cold and furious. When she finished, he was pale, his jaw set.

"*Lance* showed you that?" At her nod, he shook his head. "And he didn't tell you that it wasn't true—couldn't be true?"

"No one could have told me that."

He got up and swung away from her, his body tense. "I can see why you're hurt by what Lonigan said about you. He'll pay for it. But"—he turned and came back to her—"surely you don't believe it?"

She felt hot, angry tears sting her eyelids and furiously blinked them back. She wouldn't have believed Jonathan capable of such duplicity. "You must think I'm a fool," she said. "I've told you, Rick doesn't lie. Honesty isn't a virtue with him; he'd lie if he could get away with it. He can't, because he would be sued for libel. The item must be true."

"I see," he said, looking down at her. "Lonigan doesn't lie, and I do. Is that what you mean?"

She felt cold and hopeless. "Exactly."

His arms shot out, and his hands gripped her shoulders. "You can't believe that. You *know* me—better than anyone else does. You know how I feel—how we are, together. Do you seriously believe Lonigan's telling the truth about me?"

"Does it matter? We had only a few days more, anyway. Then I would go home, and you would head to New York with Marla."

"What makes you so sure? Suppose I prefer to stay here with you?"

She pulled away from him, crossing her arms over her breasts, rubbing her shoulders where his fingers had dug in. "You know that would be impossible," she said dully. "Why even ask? You're Jonathan Grey. I wouldn't fit into your life. I wouldn't even try. I'm not the kind of woman you need."

"Really? Are you also prepared to tell me the kind of woman I *do* need?"

"A woman like Marla, of course. She's exactly what Rick said she is—beautiful and influential. She belongs in New York; she belongs in your life. You thought so yourself until she allied herself with Rick Lonigan to find you." She hesitated. "She wasn't to blame for that, Jonathan. She simply wanted his help in finding you. I'm sure she didn't know Rick's motives."

He stared at her. "Is there no limit to your honesty? Are you trying to throw me into the arms of another woman because you think it's the right thing to do—or because you're tired of me, as Lance suggested?" He moved swiftly, catching her as she stumbled away from him, grasping her hair as she twisted her face away. His kiss was bruising and thorough. "I propose a test," he said when he took his mouth from hers. "It's a damn good way to stop an argument." He picked her up and carried her through the house to the bedroom.

She fought him, silently and desperately, while he pulled off her knitted top. His face was reddened by her blows, until finally he forced her hands behind her and held them with one of his. He yanked off her shorts and thin briefs and fell across her, pinning her to the bed with his weight, glaring at her with furious blue eyes above his flushed cheeks. "Obviously," he said grimly, "Lance was right. You are tired of me. But I'm not yet tired of you." He wrested at his belt with his free hand, surged upward long enough to unzip his slacks. "But I may be tired of you after this." Efficiently, he pushed his clothes down his lean flanks and kicked them away. "But I doubt it."

He still held her hands with his, knotted beneath her. The weight of their bodies pressed her hands deep into the mattress, immobile and helpless. Kicking was impossible; her thighs were pinioned by his hips. She shut her eyes against his glare and set her jaw, breathing hard from both exertion and anger. "You really are a bastard," she said through clenched teeth. "You got yourself into this trouble, and you're taking it out on me!"

"Naturally. What else can you expect from a liar, a cheat?" He leaned forward and pressed his mouth to hers, and she turned her head to one side, rigidly. "Oh? You refuse me your lips?" he taunted her. "Luckily, I have other choices ... With your arms behind you, your lovely breasts have risen up to meet me most invitingly." She gasped as his mouth closed over one upthrust breast, his tongue curling around the tip, tugging. "Oh, God," she whispered, "Jonathan, please ..."

"The other one? Certainly, my pleasure."

Tears squeezed from the corners of her tightly shut eyes as she tried to resist the spreading flame, the melting ache of desire. She fought her feelings angrily, keeping her body stiff, panting with the effort. But as he continued his seductive magic, her breasts seemed to expand under his moving mouth, to swell and throb against his lips.

His weight, the heat of his skin, his hard passion, were so familiar, so well loved. When he moved his knee to pry her thighs apart she could not resist, and when his mouth moved to her parted lips she sighed and yielded, her body arching to meet his thrust. It was only later, when she came slowly back from the deep dream of completion, when the beating drums of pleasure were receding in the distance, that she realized her arms were no longer beneath her, that, in fact, they were wrapped around him tightly, holding him as if she would never let go.

Chapter 14

THERE WAS NO further argument, only a rather triumphant statement from Jonathan. "As tests go," he said, still holding her tightly, "that one produced amazingly conclusive results. You aren't tired of me. Can we forget Lance's idiocy for a few hours? I'd like to go for a swim with you. And I brought home lobster to broil for dinner. This was supposed to be a vacation from trouble, remember?"

Impossible to summon back anger with her cheek pressed against his chest, feeling the vibration of his still-thumping heart. Better to push the thought of Rick's hurtful, cruel words to the back of her mind until the time came to leave. She sat up and smiled. "It's daylight," she said. "We can wear our suits and still be legal."

His laughter, she thought, was as much in relief as in appreciation of her nonsense.

She didn't mention Rick's column again. She let her world narrow to the space around them, the feeling between them, and it was enough. Beautiful, warm, and satisfying. They swam for hours, showered, and brought Max and Cabot into the kitchen to feed them, watched as their pets ran back down the steps together to disappear beneath the house.

"They're both crazy," Lacey said. "They seem to like each other better than they like us."

"Maybe they feel left out, lately." Jonathan was split-

145

ting the lobster, cleaning it, his hands deft and sure. He smiled at her as she came back from the door. "They probably sit down there sympathizing with each other, wondering how to catch our attention."

She laughed. "You're as crazy as they are." She began making salad at the counter beside him. "I suppose I am, too."

He looked at her with a faint frown. "Suspicious again? I could explain it all, if I wanted to break my word. Under the circumstances, I'd be justified. But I'm not going to, not yet."

"That isn't what I meant," Lacey said, watching him place the lobster halves on the broiler rack. "But since you brought it up, why won't you explain?"

He straightened, his broad mouth flattening. "From you, I want faith. It may be unreasonable, but I want you to believe me without explanation, without question. I *need* that."

She looked away from him, resisting the warm impulse to say she did believe him and give him the faith he wanted. But it wouldn't be true. She had needs herself, and one of them was to have her questions answered. "Let's bury that subject," she suggested. "It's too heavy."

In a minute, his face cleared. "Right. We'll enjoy the present. I'll work on the future later..."

The scent of broiling lobster began to tantalize, and she brought out a bottle of white wine, smiling as she poured it and the bouquet rose to mingle with the other appetizing smells. "Your cooking," she said, handing him a wineglass, "is even better than Rolf's."

He laughed, taking the glass and sipping, watching her over the rim with warm appreciation. "I had to produce a gourmet dinner," he said, "since I promised to take you out. I should have, I know — but I hate to share you with anyone at all."

She smiled. "No gourmet restaurant could compete with you, anyway." She was glad he didn't want to go. Now that she had succeeded in imagining this place as their own small world, the thought of others was an intrusion. "But you can take me out, after dark. For a swim." She watched him, thinking how different his craggy, stern face looked when he grinned. His teeth were so white in his bronzed face, and she loved the way his eyes lighted up...

That night, a pale, late moon rose through wisps of cloud over the dark sea as they slept naked on a blanket spread on the beach. The wan light and the encroachment of a flood tide that foamed up to touch their feet wakened them. They leaped up, shivering, to shake the sand from the blanket and run to the house, spurting with laughter like guilty children. Washed of sand and salt, they bedded down warmly in the house and slept, curled together, until the sun was high. Jonathan scrambled from bed with an oath.

"It's late," he said accusingly. "I have to be in Governor's Harbour at ten. I told Lance I'd call him."

"I hope he answers," Lacey said mildly, "instead of coming here."

"He won't come here. And he'd better have the right answer." He dressed rapidly, stamped his feet into loafers. "I'll make coffee."

The fantasy of their own little world was slipping away. Lacey dressed, wishing there were no problem with Lance Randall, wishing there were no Lance Randall, with his handsome, spoiled face and city sophistication.

By the time she was drinking Jonathan's excellent coffee, he was ready to go, stopping to give her a kiss fragrant with after shave.

"Keep Max around," he said. "You can always put him on guard if you want."

She looked after him, astounded. She had been on her own so long it was a surprise to have someone worry about her—but it was nice. She wondered suddenly if he worried about Marla.

Later, walking on the beach with Max, she still had the feeling that their time here was ending. Jonathan wanted something from Lance—some decision, or action—and somehow she knew that as long as they stayed here Lance would put it off. She remembered the way Lance had looked as he left, stubborn and petulant. Whatever Jonathan had demanded of him, Lance didn't want to do it.

She had just arrived back at the house when Jonathan drove in and came pounding up the back steps.

"Pack up," he said savagely. "Lance has weaseled out again."

She packed, knowing it was no use to ask what had happened. In less than an hour, they had eaten a hasty lunch, had loaded animals and bags into the small car. Jonathan was fired with purpose, eager to be off. He stared at Lacey impatiently as she paused at the car door and looked back. She smiled at him as she got in. "I want to remember it."

"It will still be here when we come back." He whirled the car around and into the lane, relaxing now that they were on their way. "If you refuse to return, I'll kidnap you again."

She smiled faintly, thinking how impossible that would be once they had parted and were living their own lives. But, still determined to keep things light, she remarked that she probably wouldn't put up much of a fight, and lapsed into silence.

They had passed Governor's Harbour and were driving down the sharp drop from the town before Jonathan spoke again.

"We were friends," he said, frowning. "That's hard to forget. I keep wondering if I've pushed him too hard..." He glanced at her puzzled face and gave a short laugh. "I've been with you so much that I expect you to read my mind. I was thinking of Lance. A mistake on my part, and I'll stop." He leaned back, making an effort to relax, and began pointing out things that might be of interest to her. "We can't hurry this part of the trip. When they say forty-five miles an hour on Eleuthera, they mean it."

She didn't mind. She hated leaving. It felt very much

like the beginning of the end. She thought of the first days on *The Hideout*, when she had made her determined and useless efforts to escape, and, inevitably, wondered if it would have been better if she had. She pushed all thoughts of the past away and squirmed around in the seat to look at Max, sitting at attention in the back, his long muzzle thrust forward as he watched the road ahead. Cabot, curled comfortably against the dog's flank, slept soundly. She smiled and turned around again.

"I'll have to buy Cabot a puppy," she said. "He'll be lost without Max."

"Leave him with us until you come back," Jonathan said, his eyes on the road. "He's no trouble. And Max would miss him, too."

There it was again. Until you come back... the next time... when we're here again... Perhaps he planned to take another cruise next spring or early summer, after his stint of painting. Maybe he could do that, pick up where they had left off, maintain a relationship of fun and sun without becoming involved—but she couldn't. That was something she had found out when she was with Rick. When she had tried to talk to him about his work or his life, Rick had told her she was trying to get too close—to get inside him. He had said it was a kind of intimacy he didn't want or need. "Content yourself with the outside of my body, woman," Rick had said. "Leave the rest alone." His lovemaking had mirrored that; he was selfish and superficial in bed, and wanted no more from her, either. She thought suddenly that she had been lucky, very lucky, to see it so soon, to have known instinctively that she needed more, that she had to get away from him.

"Long thoughts?"

She gave Jonathan a startled smile. "Long-ago thoughts," she corrected. "Full of thanksgiving."

"Like what?"

"Like something I'm not going to tell you. I can have secrets, too."

"My secrets will be aired, soon." He slanted her a

wry glance. "I'm already feeling exposed. You may have to comfort me."

She thought of saying she'd be glad to help, but it seemed unnecessary. He must be lonely now, at odds with Lance. Here in the islands, where he kept his identity secret, he had only a few close friends, and Lance was one of them. But in New York he must have dozens of other friends. She looked at his long fingers wrapped around the steering wheel and thought of his paintings, of the love and sensitivity, the imagination, that he put into them. Qualities that he tried to hide behind a rough masculinity and arrogance. Friends would mean a lot to him. And he would mean a lot to them, if they really understood him. She sat straighter, shaking off a sudden sadness, and began to concentrate on the scenes along the road.

The Hideout had been refueled, washed down, thoroughly cleaned inside and out. A note in the cabin informed Jonathan that both engines checked out except for one clogged fuel filter, which had been replaced. He leaped from the boat and went to find Victor Kerr, to pay him. Later, easing out of the small harbor, he told Lacey she would be more comfortable below once they were past the shallow reef.

"There's enough breeze to put up a chop," he added. "Enough to make for a wet ride. And I'm going to run. I want to make harbor in Nassau before dark."

"Shall I come up to watch for you?"

"I won't need help. If I put her up on top, the trip will be comparatively short." He stood, flexing his big shoulders. "There's no speed limit out here, and *The Hideout* and I both need the exercise. Take Max and the cat below with you, out of the spray."

When the end of the blue river was in sight, she rose obediently and went below, picked up Cabot and called Max to follow. She shut the door of the lounge behind the three of them and curled up in a chair, listening to the rising rumble of the engines as they picked up speed, feeling the faster vibration. The rumble grew to a subdued roar, and the yacht seemed to strain, pushing its lifted bow against the sea. As the roar increased, the massive stern rose suddenly and the bow dropped. Leveling off, gaining tremendous speed, the yacht ran smooth and free in winging clouds of spray. They seemed enclosed, traveling in a space of their own. Fascinated, Lacey watched through the windows and envied Jonathan his vantage point on the flying bridge. She wondered if he was wet with spray and thought he probably was and didn't care. She sighed and got up to turn on the stereo. Then she curled back into the chair and closed her eyes to listen.

Hours later, she woke, yawning, her muscles cramped. Then she realized that the boat had slowed, and got up to look. The island of New Providence lay on a darkening sea, touched with gold and red light from the sunset. She opened the door, and Max pushed past her, his coat smooth on her bare legs, and Cabot skittered after him, both of them heading for the stern. She went forward and through the saloon, climbed up until her head and shoulders were above the flying bridge deck. Damp and flushed, Jonathan grinned down at her.

"I needed that," he said. "I've been too lazy. We made time. How'd you like the ride?"

"I found it very restful. Stayed awake just long enough to find out what 'up on top' meant."

He laughed. "Break out a bottle of wine and put it in the cooler. We'll be tied up by the time it's chilled."

She dropped down into the galley and found the wine, put it in the cooler, thinking how relaxed Jonathan looked now, how companionable he was, how attractive... He would also be hungry. She looked in the refrigerator. Plenty of fresh vegetables for salad, eggs and ham for breakfast—but no dinner entrée. She went hastily to the freezer. There were thick Delmonico steaks, wrapped separately. She took out the steaks and unwrapped them, putting them on a rack to thaw. Scrubbing big baking potatoes in the small sink, she remembered that she hated to cook.

* * *

After dinner, they went to the lounge. Jonathan put a stack of records on the stereo, and as the boat rocked gently at the dock, they sat quietly in the glow from the gimbaled brass lamps. Jonathan had closed the curtains to block out the dock lights and a brightly lit, noisy party on one of the other boats. He lazed in a chair with his feet on a small table, listening to the music.

"A good dinner," he said, and groaned. "Almost too good. I thought you didn't like to cook."

"I thought so, too." She watched him through half-closed eyes as she lounged on the couch. He had showered away the salt spray and put on an old T-shirt and a soft, worn pair of jeans that outlined his muscular thighs. He looked like the man she had met in Fisherman's Cove.

"You were wrong," he said, turning his head toward her and caressing her with his eyes. Her shoulders, bare above the flame pareo she wore, felt warm from his gaze. "One can't do anything well unless one likes it. You must love to cook."

For you. Because I love you. For a moment, the words were so clear she thought she had said them aloud, and was relieved when she realized she hadn't. They were true, of course—she thought it likely she would love him for a very long time and be painfully lonely without him—but it was hardly fair to put that kind of pressure on a man at the end of an affair. Because if she said it, she wouldn't sound casual, or careless. It would be, she thought wryly, like flinging her heart at his feet and waiting to see if he'd feel forced to pick it up—not something she would want to do to either one of them, under the circumstances. She sat up, tucking her feet under her, and smiled at him, an easy, casual smile.

"Somehow, I thought I would be sitting here alone tonight," she said, "while you went to Gambier."

"The house at Gambier is full of people," he replied, yawning. "I'm going to call Lance in the morning and meet him in town. Besides, I'm looking forward to tonight, to you, to mermaids and dolphins and all that lace, and other little luxuries, like air conditioning."

Undoubtedly, Rick and Marla were still visiting Lance. And Jonathan didn't want to see them. He wanted Lance to straighten things out, first. Lacey looked down at her hands, clasped and white-knuckled in her lap. It was less than admirable of Jonathan not to face them, not to make his apologies to Marla. But she had no right or reason to criticize him. She had had no real right to object even to that unpleasant item in Rick's column. She herself was one of Jonathan's little luxuries. Everything else was her own wishful imagination. She looked up at him, lying back with his eyes shut, replete with the dinner she had cooked, listening to the soft, sensuous music. It would be over now in a day or two. She would save her regret until then. When he glanced at her, she was smiling again.

"You look sleepy."

His face brightened. "It's a pose," he said, "calculated to make you feel secure. Inside, I'm seething with an uncontrollable passion." He sprang from the chair and turned off the stereo and the lamps, leaving only the one in the passage lighted. Then he came back and pulled her up from the couch, holding her tightly, sliding his hands down to press her closer. "Come with me," he said against her mouth. "Stay with me. I need you..."

Chapter 15

A GRAY MORNING, a sea like crinkled aluminum foil, an eastern rampart of towering, dark clouds that held back the sun. Lacey, stepping out on deck, felt misty drops fall from the cabin top to chill her bare arms, a slippery wetness under her feet. A gusting wind blew trash from an overflowing barrel at the end of the empty dock, sending paper cups rattling along the boards to fall and float in sodden rafts between the silent, moored boats. Shivering, she hurried along the deck and into the saloon, finding Jonathan with a steaming pot of coffee on the stove, cups set out and forgotten, his tousled head bent over a newspaper.

"Waiting for you," he said, "with the Sunday paper and the funnies."

Now why did that warm her heart? She hid the feeling with a show of efficiency, moving briskly to the stove, pouring coffee into the cups.

"I wanted to go to the beach on Paradise Island again before I went home," she said, making conversation as she sat down, "but obviously this isn't the day for it."

"The storm will be over in an hour or so," he said lazily, and pushed sections of newspaper toward her. "The afternoon will be bright. We can go then."

She glanced at the newspaper and saw the familiar New York logo. All the important city newspapers were flown to the islands daily for the tourists, and naturally

Jonathan would pick one from New York. Her hand went out automatically for the leisure section, and she spread it on the table beside her, reading as she sipped coffee. New shows she had never heard of, a bright entertainment column written by someone whose name she didn't recognize. The format the same as when she had contributed occasional items to it. She turned pages, reading bits and pieces. Momentarily, she was back in the old building in New York, with Rick sprawled at his desk across from hers. She turned to the back page and saw his column in its usual spot in the upper left-hand corner. She glanced through it, scanning an item about two male American tennis stars, both so handsome and virile that a European princess, unable to choose between them, was considering a ménage à trois. Then a description of a beautiful sixteen-year-old actress, apparently the reason for an aging film director's divorce. The only things that ever changed in Rick's tragicomic human dramas were the names of the actors. She folded the section to toss it aside, when an item at the bottom caught her attention.

Correction

The best of us—and of course you know who we are—make mistakes. Please disregard the recent item about famous artist Jonathan Grey and wait for a new and sensational bit of information we've been promised. Sorry, Jon, we take it all back.

She gazed at it, unbelieving. In all the time Rick had been writing his column, he had never made a retraction. People had begged for them, had offered thousands of dollars for just a line or two saying he had been misinformed; yet, greedy as he was, Rick had always refused. He had said his reputation depended on never being wrong. Numbly, she folded the paper so that the item was on top and handed the section across the table to Jonathan.

He read it, nodded, and tossed the paper on the table. "I'll give Lance high marks for that when I see him this morning," he said. "It's a beginning..." He went back to the newspaper.

She stared at him, suddenly angry. "Aren't you going to say anything more about it than that? Aren't you going to tell me how Lance persuaded Rick to retract?"

Sea-blue eyes stared back at her over the top of the paper. "I don't know how he did it."

"But you called it a beginning. A beginning of what?"

He laid the paper down. "You'll find out in time. I know it's tantalizing your reporter's nose, but you'll have to wait." He picked up the newspaper again. "Be satisfied with the retraction."

"Why?" Her voice was bitter. "I, unfortunately, was in no position to ask for it. What he said about me was true. I *am* your latest playmate, circling the islands with you, staying out of sight, being secreted away in *The Hideout!*" Somehow, all her anger had exploded to the surface; she felt left out, unimportant to him— a bit player in a drama she didn't understand. Her fury built, and she added, "I have a feeling I've overstayed my welcome. The play won't fold just because I'm not here. I'm going below to pack." She slid quickly from the bench and headed for the door.

"Lacey!"

She ignored his call, plunging down the steps to the deck, running for the lounge door with tears in her eyes. In her cabin, she slammed and locked the door, dragged her backpack from the closet as Jonathan's quick footsteps sounded in the passage. She opened dresser drawers and threw clothes haphazardly on the bed, listening to him rattling the knob.

"Lacey, unlock this door."

She began sorting heavy hiking clothes, warm pajamas, long-sleeved shirts, tears dripping on them as she worked. She brushed her cheeks angrily and kept on.

"Lacey, answer me!"

She began folding clothes to fit the pack. Then his weight crashed against the door, the frame splintered, and he was inside. He was a giant in the tiny cabin; the destruction behind him made him seem even bigger. She flinched as he snatched the clothes she was holding and threw them on the bed.

"What in hell is the matter with you? You can't leave me now!"

"I can," she said. "I will. I want to, and you have no reason to stop me." She kept her face averted to hide the tears, twisting away from his hands on her shoulders.

He took a deep breath. "I have every reason to stop you. And you have no reason to leave. Please, Lacey..."

"Don't say please, Jonathan. It's out of character." She was bitter. "You're much better at ordering—or forcing." She turned and looked at him with red, accusing eyes. "And I'm no good at being submissive. I'm tired of it. I believe that item despite Rick's retraction, you know. It's all true—just as it's true about me. Someone bribed him to retract, with the promise of something much better." She jerked away from him and picked up her clothes. "I don't want to be around when the sensational bit comes out. It's been bad enough as it is."

"Give me today."

She looked back at him, startled by the suddenly quiet tone, the odd request.

"What do you mean by that?"

"Give me a chance to straighten everything out. Today. One more day, Lacey." He stopped, staring down at her. "Can't you give me the faith I asked for—for one day? I haven't lied to you."

She wanted so desperately to believe him. "I'd like to," she said, choking. "But how can I? Why can't you tell me *now?*"

"You're asking me to break a promise," he said grimly, "and I'm asking you for faith. Which would be easier for you?"

She flung the clothes down on the bed, despising her own weakness. "Today, then. But just today..."

He smiled tightly. "Put that damn backpack away. I'm hoping you won't want to use it. I'm leaving—to put some pressure on..."

She stood looking after him, past the door hanging crazily on sprung hinges. She heard him go out, and then, clearly through the open porthole, she heard him speak to the dog, putting Max on guard. She gasped and ran after him. He was halfway up the dock when she called. He turned and came back, his thick brows raised questioningly, and she pointed at the Doberman.

"I'm supposed to have faith in you," she said, "but you have none in me. I heard you put Max on guard."

Jonathan looked at her angry face and smiled. "Step over here."

She stared at him and then, doubtfully, looked at Max, who wagged his tail. Gathering courage, she pushed past the dog's long head and stepped up on the dock. Max whined and sat down, looking at her mournfully.

"You trusted me that time," Jonathan said. "It gives me some hope."

She was unsmiling. "Why didn't he stop me?"

"He's as much yours as mine, now. I thought you knew that. He wouldn't think of growling at you. I put him on guard in case of unpleasant company, since you're alone. All right?"

"All right," she said, unwillingly, and stepped back on the boat, heading toward the saloon. The coffee in her cup was cold and bitter, matching her mood. She took it up the ladder to the flying bridge and sat there, drinking it, still tense and heartsore. She felt ashamed of her hysterical burst of temper, wished she had done nothing until Jonathan had left to meet Lance. Then she could have quietly packed, left a polite note, and taken the next plane to the States. She remembered wryly that she had spent a long, drawn-out year forgetting Rick Lonigan, a lonely time, even though she had never wanted to go back to him. Forgetting Jonathan was going to take the rest of her life. It would be best to start forgetting now...

Later, when was sun was high and hot, she went into the lounge. She tried to read, but found herself listening for Jonathan's step on the dock. The sun had brought out the usual crowds, and groups of vacationers passed continually on the docks, laughing and talking. She ignored them until she heard Max's warning growl. Someone had unwisely approached the boat too closely. She got up and went out, ready to explain.

"I wouldn't have recognized you," Marla Pomeroy said lightly. "You really look quite different in those clothes."

Tall, self-possessed, and as beautiful as Lacey remembered her, Marla stood with Rick Lonigan on the edge of the dock, not at all perturbed by Max's tense body, his rumbling growl. Beside her, Rick had moved back, trying to hide the frightened look in his eyes with a forced smile. Lacey gave him a mere flick of a glance before she turned back to Marla.

"Sorry about the dog," she said. "I didn't put him on guard this time, so I can't take him off." She was not at all sure of that—Max might accept her order—but it seemed a convenient way of keeping the conversation short.

"Lacey," Rick broke in, "did you see the retraction?"
"Yes."

He laughed nervously. "I know it must have surprised you. I always said I'd never print one...but Jonathan and Marla together convinced me."

Marla shook back her gleaming blond hair and smiled. "Don't worry about Miss Thomas, Rick. She was probably rather thrilled to be mentioned in your column, even incorrectly. *I* was the one who was embarrassed..." She looked at Lacey as one woman to another. "You can understand that, can't you? It made me look so dull and uninteresting. If I weren't so sure of Jonathan, I would have been furious. But it's working out all right. The retraction helps, and Jon and I are planning an early wedding, which will silence the whole thing." She smiled with charming friendliness. "That's why Rick and I are here. When I found out Jon had a yacht, I wanted to see it. I haven't told him yet, but I think it would be wonderful for a wedding trip. You've been living on it. Tell me, is it comfortable?"

"Very," said Lacey steadily. "Luxurious, in fact. Too bad you can't come aboard and see for yourself." She looked down at the dog. "If only you weren't on guard, Max."

At the word "guard," he thrust his nose through the rail and growled ominously. Lacey forced a rueful smile. "You see how it is," she said. "There'll be another time, of course."

Marla nodded. "Many of them, I'm sure. It's truly a lovely yacht." She turned and hooked a hand in Rick's arm. "We really should be going. Jonathan has so little time these days, and he'll be looking for us."

They moved away, unhurriedly, looking curiously at the other yachts and sailing craft. Their tall, fashionable figures shimmered in Lacey's blurred gaze. Beside her, Max had stopped guarding. The threat had passed, and he leaned contentedly against her thigh. She dropped a hand to his head in a brief caress and turned swiftly to the lounge door.

It took longer to write the note to Jonathan than it had taken to pack. Her first drafts were bitter, mentioning Marla and Rick. Her pride intervened when she realized he would know she was hurt. She tried another and another, but none of them hid her feelings well enough to suit her, and, frantic because of the time, she finally left only a curt, scribbled message: "Thanks for the fun, and best wishes, Lacey."

She caught a taxi at the end of the marina docks, and at the airport found a cancellation open on a plane that was loading. Forty-five minutes after she left the yacht, she landed in Palm Beach and took the next bus north to Tarpon City, Cabot growling in his carrier.

It was only a block from the bus station to the garage where her car waited. At her apartment, Bert and Marie Andrews came out to greet her, and she told them a hastily invented story about a family emergency in Vermont, picking that state because she had spent part of her childhood there and still had a distant cousin living in the area. "I have to go," she explained. "I hate to give up the apartment, but my aunt is all alone . . . I have some things to do in town now, but I'll be back later to pack."

She dumped Cabot out of his carrier into his favorite chair and left, going first to *The Clarion,* where she told Pike Farrell the same story, improving with practice. She noted that her substitute was doing a satisfactory job, picked up a few personal things she had left there, and went out, after a round of farewells during which she rather stiffly accepted sympathy for her sick aunt.

"Buck up," Pike said, alarmed. "You look too pale under that tan. You're going to get sick yourself, if you worry too much. And come back when you can. Your job will be waiting."

She thanked him and left, going to the bank, where she closed out her account, taking half of the money in traveler's checks. In answer to the teller's question, she told him that she had no idea when she might return.

During the late afternoon, she worked fast, driving herself, needing to get away from the sight of the bay sparkling in the sunlight. She had told Bert Andrews that she had sold the canoe at the garage, but while she packed things for storage she thought of the slim, yellow shape in the mangrove thicket on Fisherman's Cove. She wondered if the clinging, tentacle roots of the mangroves would grow around it in time, would hold the canoe prisoner so that it would never escape to float, buoyant and inviting, on the water of the bay. She hoped a storm would come and wash it out before the roots tightened, and that someone would find it.

She was ready to leave shortly after dark. There hadn't been that much to pack into the car, and Marie and Bert had helped, sympathetic and worried. At last, she carried Cabot to the car and tossed him, free, into the back seat.

"If you can behave in a car with Max, you can behave with me," she told him. "Any shenanigans, and you go in here." She brandished the carrier at him, and he sat down primly on the seat and began washing a paw.

Bert and Marie came out again as she started the car.

"You ought to wait until morning to start," Bert told her. "You look real tired. I know you're worried about your aunt, but—"

"I'll be fine," Lacey interrupted, ashamed of worrying them. "Really I will. I'm tough."

"Write," said Marie, "just so we'll know you got there."

She promised, and drove away. She was out of Florida and passing across the Georgia line into South Carolina before she acknowledged to herself that she was not truly escaping. The pain and loneliness were traveling with her.

By the end of the second week in Vermont, Lacey knew she wasn't tough. She had wandered from one small town to another, looking for a job that would keep her. Salaries for women reporters seemed to be geared exclusively to those who lived with their parents or were only augmenting a husband's pay. So she continued to move on, but with decreasing hope of finding employment in Vermont. She had sent a postcard to Marie and Bert Andrews when she arrived, and since she had forgotten by then whether she had a sick aunt or a sick cousin, she had said only that her "patient" was better but still sick and lonely, which seemed a good description of the only patient she had—herself. The lonely part, was especially true, so she ended up heading for New York, where at least she had friends.

She arrived on a pleasant, bright Sunday morning when she knew Shelley Parker would be at home. Shelley was a natural homemaker and spent every weekend cleaning her small apartment until it shone. Lacey found a phone booth and, her heart quickening at the thought of a friendly voice, called.

Shelley squealed with genuine delight. "Come right up here—now! I can't wait to see you. Do you still have that crazy cat? Bring him, too. And, oh—I'll call Eileen..."

"Please, no," Lacey said. "Just you."

"Oh-h?" Pleasure at being chosen colored Shelley's voice. "Just us two? Great. I'll make a casserole..."

When Lacey arrived, Shelley embraced her warmly, her round face pink with excitement. She led Lacey to a chair in the small living room while Cabot stalked away to find a sunny place to sit. Shelley plumped down beside Lacey and gave her a look electric with curiosity.

"You're a celebrity, Lacey! Imagine being mentioned in 'VIPs and Quips' and then getting the first-ever retraction! Eileen is dying of curiosity, but then, so am I. Was it the real Jonathan Grey that Lonigan thought was your lover, or the other one?"

Lacey stared at her. "What do you mean? Is there more than one?"

"Of course! Haven't you read the papers? The man everyone thought was Jonathan Grey wasn't Grey at all." Her blue eyes sparkled as she added blithely, "Somone else was, naturally."

"Oh, come on, Shelley. Who said so?"

"Why, he did! Grey. I mean the fake one. He confessed in 'VIPs and Quips' that he was just Grey's agent. He told a long story about how it happened, but what it boiled down to was that when the first buyers saw Grey's name on the paintings, they assumed the agent had painted them himself, and he let them think so. He said Grey found out after a time, but that he didn't care. He didn't want to be a celebrity, anyway—just wanted to bum around in the Bahamas and paint."

"Lance Randall," Lacey said slowly.

"Then you did know! That's the fake's real name, and wow—is he ever gorgeous. Was he the one you were with?"

Lacey shook her head. "I was with—I mean, I know the real one." It was impossible to take all this in at once, but she was hurting already, afraid to hear more.

"Oh." Shelley's face dropped. *"He* doesn't even seem

like an artist. Big and rough-looking." She sighed. "I guess it's just as well, though. You might have really fallen in love with the handsome one, and he's out of circulation. He's married to Marla Pomeroy. Didn't you know the Pomeroys? They own the gallery..."

"I know," Lacey said tiredly. *And I know whom Marla meant when she said she was engaged to Jonathan Grey. I know whom Rick quoted in those items. I know a lot of things I wish I didn't know, too. Like what a fool I've been. Jonathan asked me to trust him, and I didn't. How he must hate me now.* She looked at Shelley and tried to smile. "What did the real Jonathan Grey have to say?"

"Not much," Shelley said carelessly. "Except that it was all true, and that Randall would continue to be his representative." She stared at Lacey. "Are you all right?"

"Just surprised."

"But you were there! It must have been exciting. What happened, anyway?"

There was no way to tell just part of it, and there was no way she could bear to tell it all. She looked at Shelley. "Are you going to be mad if I don't tell you anything?" She had forgotten how transparent Shelley was. She watched emotions chase themselves across the clear eyes. Surprise, disappointment, a dawning sympathy.

Shelley leaned over and took her hand. "Oh, Lacey," she said softly, "you've been hurt. That Rick—he got you into it. You used to say he was a demon."

She could say it hadn't been Rick's fault, but then she would have to say more. Lacey sighed.

"I just want to forget it all," she told Shelley. "I need to find a job, a place to live."

"Everything's rented," Shelley said, "and all the rents are astronomical. Including mine. I've been looking for— hey! Why not share my place? I have to find a roommate to help pay the rent, and you'd be the very best. Please!"

Lacey's laugh was shaky. "Looks as if my luck has turned," she said wryly.

That night she lay in Shelley's immaculate apartment, sleepless. Just one day, Jonathan had said. One day to clear everything up. And she had promised him that one day. One day of the faith he wanted, to prove he hadn't lied to her. Ruefully, she thought that while she had survived, so far, what felt like a broken heart, it was possible that she might die of regret.

The third day in New York Lacey had a job. She had known it would take only a telephone call to be back at her old desk, working with Rick, but she didn't want that—or, for that matter, anything else connected with newspapers. So she mailed in résumés and applications for various technical writing jobs that had been listed in the classified ads, and prepared to wait. Bored, she had gone to find something to read at a family-owned bookstore that had been one of her favorite haunts and found that the assistant manager was leaving to have a baby. The owners greeted her with open arms and gave her the position.

"It's great," she told Shelley that evening. "I love to read, and now it's part of my job. The saleswomen are eager and pleasant, both of them, and the customers seem to be super. What more could I ask?"

"Not a thing," Shelley assured her, putting a steaming casserole on the table, "unless it would be a handsome, book-loving man to wander in. Single, of course." Her blue eyes were wistful. "If there *are* any single ones..."

"I'll bring him home," Lacey promised. "Once he tastes your cooking, he won't be single long." Living with Shelley, she had realized just how nice her friend really was. Some man would find out, and then Lacey would be looking for another roommate, or living alone with Cabot. Jonathan had said she'd never make it as an old maid—but maybe for once he'd been wrong.

They took turns buying groceries. A week later, shopping in a neighborhood store, Lacey heard a smothered but enthusiastic yelp.

"Lacey! It's really you!"

Eileen, eyes sparkling, red mouth curving, was staring at her. Her dark hair hung over the shoulders of a good-looking business suit. She looked vibrant and happy and completely surprised. She came teetering over on her spike heels to throw her arms around Lacey's shoulders and then stand back to look her over.

"Are you ever skinny, my friend," Eileen said. "But it's becoming. You look gorgeous. Wait until I tell Rick you're back. I swear he's still mooning over you. Where are you staying?"

"With Shelley," Lacey said, resigned. If she didn't tell her, Eileen would call Shelley anyway. "But don't tell Rick, please. I'm not eager to see him."

"Oh? Well, then I won't." Eileen cocked her head, curious and demanding. "But I'm coming over. I've got to hear about this Bahamas adventure of yours, every detail of it. You really had a fantastic time, didn't you?"

"Probably too fantastic to be believed, if you've been listening to Rick," Lacey said. "Frankly, I've been trying to forget it. How was the camping trip?"

"Like always, of course—fun but not exciting. I'll tell you about it later. Right now, I've got to rush..."

Lacey watched her go, knowing Eileen would tell Rick of their encounter. Walking back to the apartment with her bag of groceries, she decided her friend's "rush" was probably to the nearest telephone. That evening, she knew she had been right. Shelley answered the downstairs bell and came back with a worried expression on her round face.

"It's Rick Lonigan," she said. "He knows you're here. What shall I say?"

"Tell him to come up," Lacey said wryly. It had been inevitable. Sooner or later, Rick would have discovered she was in town. Even New York wasn't big enough, when he knew so many of her friends. She exchanged the silky robe she had put on with a relaxing evening in mind, for dark slacks and a turtleneck pullover. She heard Rick's voice in the living room, friendly and assured, and heard Shelley laugh, sounding pleased. She grimaced. Rick could put anyone at ease when he tried. It was part of his stock in trade. He never forgot that even ordinary people could be sources of gossip if they liked you.

He smiled as she came into the room and quickly put an arm around her shoulders. "Looking great, kid," he said, and led her to the couch, sinking down beside her.

"Eileen told me you didn't want to see me—so I didn't call ahead." His voice was humorous, inviting her to laugh with him. She managed a smile, watching Shelley slip from the room diplomatically.

"Very intelligent," she said. "Now, tell me why you wanted to see me."

"Don't you know? You were the prettiest assistant I ever had, and I want you back again. Badly." There was a note of pleading in his voice, and she looked at him in astonishment.

"Sorry." She moved slightly, putting distance between them. "I've got a job I like better."

"And a man you like better?"

She wondered what she had ever seen in him. "Let's leave the past alone, Rick. What we had—and it wasn't much—disappeared a long time ago."

"It wouldn't have—if I could have found you. I thought at first you'd come back. When you didn't, I tried to find you. But I didn't have a clue as to where you'd gone until you called Eileen about that camping trip."

"A mistake on my part. But I thought, after a year..." She stopped, seeing that the conversation was leading nowhere. "Forget it, Rick. I'm just not interested."

"You're still angry about what I wrote, aren't you?"

"No."

His thin mouth twisted. "I retracted—something I promised myself I would never do. But the man I thought was Jonathan Grey promised me a blockbuster story if I did, and Marla threatened to sue me if I didn't. I really thought the guy was seeing you; he was gone so often, and I knew—or thought I knew—that it was his yacht you were on. I wouldn't have written that item with so little to go on... except that I was jealous." He laughed. "Crazy. The whole time, you really were with Jonathan

Grey, the real one." He looked at her speculatively. "What a story that would have made—the two of you dodging around, keeping his identity hidden. It would still be a good story. Listen, if you'll just cooperate, I'll give you full credit in the column..."

"Oh, shut up," she said, disgusted. "Don't you ever stop digging up gossip? So that's why you want me back!"

"No, it isn't." He reached for her, trying to put his arms around her unyielding body. "I want you back on any terms..."

She pulled away from him and stood up. "No terms, not even a truce. I'm just not coming back. You didn't believe Eileen, but maybe you'll believe me. I don't want to see you again."

His knowing eyes narrowed as he rose from the couch. "I see I guessed right," he said. "You're set on higher stakes, aren't you? Well, if you want Grey to find you, you'd better put yourself in his path before he stops looking. There are a lot of women oohing and ahhhing over him now."

Silent, she watched him go to the door and let himself out. He turned before he closed it and gave her his sardonic grin. "Don't forget, kid. Vermont... New York... A man can get tired of looking. Grey went back to the tropics, I guess. Maybe he's already found someone else."

She stood there, shaken. It was like Rick to be cruel—especially when she had just turned him down. He had sensed it would hurt her to bring up Jonathan's name. But the mention of Vermont had brought a tiny, flickering hope. Had Jonathan actually been searching for her? Was he still interested, after everything that had happened? No one knew she had gone to Vermont except Shelley, and Bert and Marie Andrews. She shook her head. It was considerably more likely that Rick, who had already met Bert and Marie, had gone there to ask where she had gone... and had mentioned it only to give her false hope. It was typical of him to take revenge that way.

That night she dreamed, as she often did, of the yellow canoe and the mangrove-bordered cove. Of herself, paddling toward the little beach, and the big Doberman standing there wagging his tail. She woke with a start just as the bow of the canoe touched sand, and wondered afterward if the dream meant that she was too much a coward to face Jonathan again, to take the chance that he might not be at all pleased to see her.

But what Rick had said stayed with her, and at noon she made a long-distance call to Florida. Marie Andrews was delighted to hear from her and asked immediately about her aunt.

"My aunt? Oh, she's fine." She had forgotten the nonexistent aunt. "I'm working in New York now. I— I just thought I'd call. I miss you both, and... and I was wondering, you know... about mail, or if anyone had called..."

"The bills you told us about came, and we paid them with the money you left," said Marie practically, "but there haven't been any telephone calls that I know of." She laughed. "One visitor, though—a big man who asked so many questions I thought he was from the IRS. Bert told him we didn't have your address in Vermont, but he gave him your parents' California address—where we sent your things for storage."

Lacey thanked her and hung up. Her fingers trembling, she dialed her parents' California number.

"Dad?"

"Lacey? Well, it's about time you got in touch. We found out over a month ago that you'd left Florida, and your mother has done nothing but fret because she didn't know where you were. Why didn't you let us know?"

"I'm sorry. I'm breaking in a new job in New York... but how did you find out I moved?"

"For one thing, we got all your knickknacks to store, but before that some friend of yours called, trying to get your address. He said you'd left Florida for Vermont. Let's see, I can't remember his name—Mother talked to him..." His voice receded and then came back. "She says Grey—John Grey, she thinks. Anyway, she wants to talk to you..."

"Why ever did you go to Vermont, dear?" came her mother's inquisitive voice. "Did you go to see your cousin? When Mr. Grey said he was trying to find you, I gave him Anna Maria's address. Did he find you?"

"No. No, he didn't."

"Then I hope it wasn't important. Now, I have a pencil and notebook right here, and I want your address. You know you should always..."

Lacey listened, impatient but warmed by her parents' concern and love. She had neglected them, she knew, but she hated taking trouble to her parents. She waited for a break in the flow of words and then asked for her cousin's address and phone number. "I might go up there again sometime, and drop in on her," she added weakly, knowing she wouldn't. But she had to call Anna Maria—immediately.

Anna Maria was surprisingly informative. "No, he didn't call. He came here! He's a friend of yours? He looks like a big pirate, with that deep tan and the scowl on his face. I told him I hadn't seen you in years, not since we were children, and he left. But he called back a week or so later, to see if you'd arrived since. He said then that he had checked newspaper offices all over the state. Do you work on a newspaper, Lacey?"

Lacey said she used to, but not anymore, and exchanged family news for a few minutes. She gave Anna Maria her address, in case Jonathan called again.

But he wouldn't, she thought as she hung up. He had come to a dead end in Vermont; he wouldn't go there again. Rick had said he'd gone back to the tropics. Well, there was no telephone at the old house, and he wouldn't be there in any case. He'd done his paintings for the year. She thought of *The Hideout,* cruising the innumerable cays and islands of the Bahamas, and knew that he had escaped her as well as the rest of the world. There was only one chance. She picked up the telephone one more time, called the club at Eleuthera, and asked for Victor Kerr.

"Wictah Kahh 'ere. Yes, 'e was, miss, but 'e left a veek past. A short wisit and gone..."

"When he comes back, will you give him my address?"

She repeated the address twice, and had Victor read it back to make sure he had it right. Then she hung up and went back to work, somehow surprised to find herself in New York when moments before she had been in Eleuthera. Talking to Victor had brought it back so clearly.

Chapter 16

AFTER A MONTH, Lacey was sure Jonathan was no longer interested in her. He would surely have been back to Eleuthera by now, and Victor Kerr was dependable. He wouldn't have forgotten to give Jonathan her address.

It was better to know, she told herself, so she could put him out of her mind. She concentrated on her work at the bookstore, liking it better every day. Eileen came by and took her out to lunch, in a sort of apology for having broken her promise not to tell Rick.

"You really burned Rick," she said, eyeing Lacey with wary respect. "I don't know why he's taking it out on me. I told him you didn't want to see him."

"I know you told him I was in town, Eileen," Lacey said, "and it's all right. I suppose I had to talk to Rick one last time, and I'm glad it's over with now."

They left the restaurant companionably in the fine fall weather, and in front of the bookstore Eileen clasped her hand warmly. "You're getting your color back, Lacey," she said. "You looked a bit peaked. Losing your tan, I suppose. When are you going to tell me about your Bahamian adventure?"

"I've forgotten it all," Lacey lied, "but if you like stories, I'm selling books in here..." She forced a smile as Eileen backed off, laughing. Would it ever stop hurting to be reminded?

She had started reading the newspapers again. A few days later, an item in Rick's column arrested her attention; her heart was pounding as she finished it. Lance Randall and his wife, the former Marla Pomeroy, now comanagers of the Pomeroy Gallery, were launching the fall season with a special showing of some new paintings by Jonathan Grey. "These pictures are completely different from Grey's past works, we hear," Rick had written, "but Marla says they're clearly among his best. Exciting, she calls them, and beautiful. Evidently Grey hasn't lost his touch since he came out of hiding..."

He followed that with a summary of what he called Jonathan's "Bahamian statement," going over the years when Grey had been hidden from the public and Lance Randall had been what he called "Grey's glorified proxy." Lacey put the paper down, thrilled over the news but dully angry at Rick. Would he ever let it alone? So Lance and Marla were working together, making a life of their own. It was surprisingly heartwarming to discover that Marla had really loved Lance, not just his cachet as a famous artist. But the thought of Jonathan's new paintings overrode other thoughts. She could not stop thinking about the showing.

In the following days, her defenses crumbled. The door she had shut in her memory opened, and everything tumbled out—the old house and the draped easel, the golden days and turquoise seas, Jonathan's vivid blue eyes with the bronze skin crinkled around them as he laughed. And constantly, achingly, she recalled the ecstasy of their lovemaking. She pushed the memories back, but they tumbled out again, as if they had a life and will of their own.

She found herself looking forward to reading the newspaper every morning, searching through it for articles about the opening of Jonathan's new show. Her tension grew, and with it came indecision. She longed to see the paintings; yet now that Jonathan was known as the artist, he would undoubtedly be present at the show, at least during the first few days. He would be doing the things he hated—attending receptions, greeting the serious collectors—the things Lance had done so well for him. She could see him in the press of a typical reception at the gallery, balancing a cocktail glass in one hand, towering over the crowd, trying to make small talk with the fashionable sophisticates who attended such affairs. His eyes would be strained, searching for escape. It saddened her, though she knew she wouldn't see it. If she went to the show at all, it would be near the closing day. All the social events would be over by then, and Jonathan wouldn't be there.

The day the first article appeared she decided she wouldn't go at all. It had only been a week since she had read about the show in Rick's column, yet she realized that thinking about it—which she did constantly—had reopened wounds, wakened impossible dreams and vain regret. She wasn't sleeping well, and her new life seemed dull. It would be worse, she thought, if she saw the paintings, and read Jonathan's thoughts in them, which she knew she would. Still, she scanned the article, skipping to the quotations from the gallery's new managers: "We are proud to present Image of Love, Jonathan Grey's triumphant departure from his usual style... a realistic celebration of life and human emotion..." The article went on, in resounding phrases, and Lacey scanned it quickly, seeing that the opening would take place in two days, that the paintings would be on view for only a few weeks. She folded the paper and put it away, thinking that soon it would be over and she would be able to put the past aside again and get on with the business of living. Until then, she knew that the show would dominate her thoughts.

Four days later, perched on a ladder taking books from a top shelf, she heard the door open and looked down at a tall, blond woman who seemed vaguely familiar even from a top view. She climbed down, bringing an armload of books, ready to greet the customer politely.

"I found you," said Marla. "Believe me, it hasn't been easy." She was smiling, friendly, and full of her usual self-confidence. She reached out and took the books from Lacey's nerveless hands and put them down on a counter.

"I want a word with you—I should say, several words."

"How did you find me?" Seeing Marla had shaken her badly. "How did you know I was in New York?"

"I was always sure you'd come back to New York eventually," Marla said. "But the rest of it was sheer feminine intuition." Her smile widened. "That rat Lonigan has been going around looking like a cat with a mouthful of canary feathers, and he knew we'd been searching for you. I finally pinned him down, and he admitted he'd seen you, and told me where you were living. I saw Shelley Parker an hour ago and persuaded her to tell me where you worked. So, here I am. Now, why haven't you been to our show?"

Blood burned up into Lacey's pale face. "Well, I—I thought about it," she said, her voice shaking. Then, in a rush, she added, "Marla, I didn't think I could stand it. I'm trying to forget—everything." She looked up at Marla's self-assured face helplessly. "I'm glad things turned out well for you and Lance."

"Turned out great," Marla said. "I learned a few things about reality, and Lance did, too. He's beginning to appreciate his own very real abilities. We're working like beavers together and loving every minute of it." She paused, looking at Lacey speculatively. "I really want you to see the show. If you won't come by yourself, I'll take you."

"Why? I mean, why is it important for me to see it? I certainly don't have the money to buy a Jonathan Grey painting." She was regaining some of her poise, but not nearly enough. Her voice still shook as she said his name.

"Various reasons," Marla said vaguely. "You often attended the important shows at the gallery, and I want your opinion of the way we've mounted Jon's work. This is the first show that Lance and I have put together. Don't you want to see how we've done?"

"Of course I'd like that; I really wish you both well. But I..." She couldn't bring herself to tell Marla that she couldn't take the chance of seeing Jonathan, of watching his sea-blue eyes turn cool and reserved. "I work, as you can see. I'm alone here today, and I can't leave the store..." That wasn't true. One of the clerks was in the back room, unpacking a carton of books. But Marla didn't know that, and perhaps she would stop insisting.

"Not to worry." Marla was smiling again. "I'll come by at closing time and pick you up. The gallery will be closed by then. You can see the paintings without the crowds."

In spite of her feelings, Lacey capitulated. "All right. That's really nice of you." She felt relieved, as if the matter had been taken out of her hands, and she did want to see the show. In Marla's company, she could be more objective, more poised. "The new paintings must be super, for you to go to so much trouble."

"You'll see," Marla said, her eyes sparkling. "They'll knock you for a loop." She left, her long legs striding with an air of mission accomplished.

The feeling of relief and happiness lasted. As Lacey went back to work, she realized that underneath all her fears she wanted nothing more than to see Jonathan's work, and was glad Marla had forced her to make a decision. She was also glad that it would be after regular hours when she arrived. She had worn a pair of old jeans to the store, knowing that she was going to spend the day on the ladder, and the white silk shirt she had on had certainly seen better days. Not the kind of clothing one wore to the Pomeroy Gallery—but there would be no one there to notice.

By closing time, she had finished stacking the high shelves and rolled the ladder out of the way. In the small bathroom at the rear of the shop, she washed the dust from her hands and face and combed her hair. She could see the excitement building in her eyes, which seemed huge in her too-pale face, and she took out a lipstick to add a touch of color. When Marla arrived in a cab, Lacey locked the store, suddenly lighthearted. It would be wonderful to see the show—and she could worry about forgetting it later.

As the cab edged its way uptown, Marla told her that most of the paintings were already sold, which was usual with a Grey show. "Prices you wouldn't believe," she added triumphantly. "Our commission on them is more than the asking price on most paintings." She looked at Lacey and laughed. "Of course, we haven't allowed them to be removed yet. You'll see them all."

Lacey nodded, understanding Marla's triumph. Having taken over management of the gallery, naturally she and Lance would want it to be successful. And Jonathan would be pleased. At least her discovery of the old house hadn't torn up his life—as he had said it would.

The big windows of the Pomeroy Gallery were dark, the carriage lights on either side of the oak door gleaming in the twilight as they got out of the taxi.

"Advantages of knowing the management," Marla said, laughing, as she unlocked and then opened the door. "A private showing." They went down a dimly lit hall to the main room where the work of important artists was shown, and Marla searched out the switches, finally finding the right ones. Then the big room sprang to life around them. Indirect cove lighting circled the walls, with track lights spotlighting each painting. There were five of them.

Lacey gasped, and then let her breath out slowly. "No..."

"Yes." Marla's voice was soft. "The name of the show should have told you." She pushed her forward. "Start with that one—with the canoe..."

Lacey's first sweeping look had told her. They were all portraits, all full length, and all of her. Huge, glowing, detailed... how could he remember so well? She went slowly toward the closest one.

The canoe floated on the surface of the cove, and she knelt in it, with the paddle in her hands, the sun across her face. She was wide-eyed and beautiful... more beautiful by far than she really was, or ever had been. Mangroves dipped to the water behind the canoe, glistening green. Her eyes were questioning, doubtful. Lacey remembered it—remembered her fear of him. She glanced back at Marla, who still leaned in the doorway, and went on to the next picture.

This Lacey sat cross-legged on the deck of the yacht, barefoot and dressed in rumpled hiking shorts. Her dark head was bent; only a firm chin and curve of cheek showed anything of her face. She held a gray cat in her arms, comforting the animal. The cat's yellow eyes looked up at her, asking for reassurance. Beyond the gleaming rail of the yacht, water foamed and leaped. The first day, crossing the Gulf Stream, when she had turned around and caught him watching her.

Her eyes widened as she came to the next painting. She lay in the carved bed, the mermaids and dolphins sporting above her, the frilled lace coverlet pushed below her waist. Bare breasts, rose-tipped, her sleeping face as innocent as that of a child. This one, only he could remember. She moved on, dazed and wondering.

The beach at Paradise Island. That sweep of curved sand, the blue water. Long shadows from leaning palms. And a nymph in silver-lilac, running with a huge dog that seemed to laugh, his red tongue lolling. They raced, eager and happy, through shadow into sun. She looked at this one a long time and then turned back to look again at the ones she had already seen. It was there in every brush stroke, every tender, luminous color. Passion, and love. He loved her. She wanted to shout, to make the big room echo. She swung to look at Marla, flinging her arms wide in joy, and Marla laughed softly.

"One more," she said, and motioned Lacey on.

In the final portrait, she wore a flame-red pareo that left her shoulders bare. The small couch on which she sat was easy to recognize; it was the one in the lounge of *The Hideout*. A gimbaled brass lamp shone down on her, lighting her face, accenting the curve of her breasts. She stared directly out of the painting, and to Lacey it was like looking into a mirror and seeing her own heart. Love shone naked from the gray eyes, trembled on the parted lips. It was plain that the Lacey in the portrait was watching her beloved.

Then he had known, too. He had known she loved him, at the end of the progression of their days. There was no room for doubt. She turned and walked back across the big room to Marla.

"I'm going to him," she said, "if you can tell me where he is. If not, I'll go to Eleuthera and wait."

Marla laughed, yet impossibly, her cool eyes were wet. "Idiot. Did you think he'd leave while there was a chance of finding you? He painted these pictures as bait—hoping to draw you out of hiding and show you that you two belong together. I told him I found you today and would bring you here tonight. But when I said you were hard to convince, he was afraid you might not want to see him." She paused, laughing again. "He said I'd know, because you could never hide what you felt. He was right."

"Marla," Lacey said dangerously, "tell me—now. Where he is."

"Oh, he's in my father's office, waiting. It's down the hall behind that door. You can't miss it; the light's on..."

Lacey ran down the hall, her steps echoing. Her heart caught as she saw Jonathan appear in the lighted doorway, a huge silhouette with tousled hair coming toward her. He reached out and caught her in his arms, lifting her until her face was level with his, her arms around his neck.

"Christmas morning," he said, his voice shaking. "That's what you are."

"I'm part of you," she whispered, tears in her eyes. "And I want the rest..."

He kissed her gently, first on the mouth and then on her wet cheeks. Swinging into the lighted room, he kneed the door shut and sat down with her in his lap. She clung to him, fitting herself tightly into the planes and hollows of his body, and when he tried to draw away to look at her she pulled him closer, wriggling into his solid warmth until he laughed and kissed her again, not so gently, and the heat began to rise between them. When he drew away again, his hand had found a way inside her silk shirt and pushed aside her bra. She moved, fitting her breast more fully into his hand, her eyes half-closed.

"I told you once," he said, "not to tease a hungry man."

She put her hand over his, pressing it against her. "I'm not teasing. I mean it." She opened her eyes fully and looked into his, drowning in the sea-blue depths. "I thought you'd given up on me," she said, "and I didn't blame you. I didn't give you your day—the one day you asked for..."

"Give me years, instead. Years and years, all we have..." He kissed her again, demandingly, holding her too tight for breathing. "I thought I'd lost you...I hunted everywhere..."

She struggled up and took a deep breath. "I left my address a month ago with Victor Kerr."

"But I haven't been there! I've been at the old house, painting—painting you, over and over..."

"I saw. Darling, I am *not* that beautiful."

"You are much more beautiful than that," he said with conviction. "There's something that shines through you. Something magical..."

"Oh, *that*," Lacey said, suddenly filled again with high, sure joy. "That's only love. No one sees it but you..."

"*Only* love?" he asked unsteadily. "Only, Lacey?" He rubbed his cheek against her silky hair. "Never take it away from me again."

The door behind them opened. "Sorry," Marla said sweetly, "gallery hours are over." She looked at them tangled in the chair and laughed. "Aren't you wasting time? There will always be chances to talk."

"Right," Jonathan said, "all the time we have left." He stood Lacey on her feet and got up. "Come on. We're leaving tonight."

"You'll need reservations," Marla said practically. "Night flights are popular now. Come over to our place and call from there."

Moving toward the door, pulling Lacey along, Jonathan grinned and stopped long enough to brush a kiss on Marla's cheek. "Bless you," he said. "You found her for me. But we don't need anything except a taxi. I brought *The Hideout*. She's waiting at a Long Island marina."

Outside, trying to keep up with him, Lacey was breathless. She pulled him to a stop, shivering in the cold night air. "Break, so I can breathe," she said. "And I want to ask—I understand now that you had promised Lance he could break the news that he was not Jonathan Grey, since if you did it, it would be like exposing a crime. But why do it at all? You liked being anonymous. Why didn't you keep it that way?"

"Questions." He sighed. "I see it clearly. A lifetime of questions ahead. It's simple. I wanted my name back so I could give it to you. So you wouldn't be Mrs. Anonymous." He put an arm around her, and she pressed against his warm side as they began walking again.

"Well," she said finally, "you never once said you loved me."

"You knew that, surely?" His gaze slanted down at her. "Didn't I let you seduce me all those times?" He laughed as she looked up, startled, and then stopped, wrapping her in his arms. "Ah, darling, I think I fell in love with you while I was bandaging your foot... or maybe before that, when I picked you up. But I was never quite sure of you. Now, come *on*. We have to get Cabot before we leave. Max has been half-crazy, looking for him."

In the taxi, snuggling against him and not only for warmth, Lacey became practical. "I have to pack," she said. "How can we leave tonight?"

"Just grab a sweater," Jonathan said carelessly. "You left all those clothes from Madame Li on the boat, and we can buy more in Freeport."

He had kept her clothes. Waiting, in that crazy cabin with that fancy bed bedecked with mermaids and dolphins. She sat up and stretched as the taxi slowed in front of her apartment house. She was about to break all records for quick packing. She could hardly wait to return to *The Hideout*, to golden days and turquoise seas, shared with the man she adored.

WONDERFUL ROMANCE NEWS!

Do you know about the exciting SECOND CHANCE AT LOVE/TO HAVE AND TO HOLD newsletter? Are you on our *free* mailing list? If reading all about your favorite authors, getting sneak previews of their latest releases, and being filled in on all the latest happenings and events in the romance world sounds good to you, then you'll love our SECOND CHANCE AT LOVE and TO HAVE AND TO HOLD Romance News.

If you'd like to be added to our mailing list, just fill out the coupon below and send it in... and we'll send you your *free* newsletter every three months — hot off the press.

☐ *Yes, I would like to receive your free SECOND CHANCE AT LOVE/TO HAVE AND TO HOLD newsletter.*

Name _____
Address _____
City _____ **State/Zip** _____

Please return this coupon to:

    Berkley Publishing
    200 Madison Avenue, New York, New York 10016
    Att: Irene Majuk

HERE'S WHAT READERS ARE SAYING ABOUT

Second Chance at Love®

"I think your books are great. I love to read them, as does my family."
—*P. C., Milford, MA**

"Your books are some of the best romances I've read."
—*M. B., Zeeland, MI**

"SECOND CHANCE AT LOVE is my favorite line of romance novels."
—*L. B., Springfield, VA**

"I think SECOND CHANCE AT LOVE books are terrific. I married my 'Second Chance' over 15 years ago. I truly believe love is lovelier the second time around!"
—*P. P., Houston, TX**

"I enjoy your books tremendously."
—*I. S., Bayonne, NJ**

"I love your books and read them all the time. Keep them coming—they're just great."
—*G. L., Brookfield, CT**

"SECOND CHANCE AT LOVE books are definitely the best!"
—*D. P., Wabash, IN**

*Name and address available upon request

- ___07246-X SEASON OF MARRIAGE #158 Diane Crawford
- ___07576-0 EARTHLY SPLENDOR #161 Sharon Francis
- ___07580-9 STARRY EYED #165 Maureen Norris
- ___07592-2 SPARRING PARTNERS #177 Lauren Fox
- ___07593-0 WINTER WILDFIRE #178 Elissa Curry
- ___07594-9 AFTER THE RAIN #179 Aimée Duvall
- ___07595-7 RECKLESS DESIRE #180 Nicola Andrews
- ___07596-5 THE RUSHING TIDE #181 Laura Eaton
- ___07597-3 SWEET TRESPASS #182 Diana Mars
- ___07598-1 TORRID NIGHTS #183 Beth Brookes
- ___07800-X WINTERGREEN #184 Jeanne Grant
- ___07801-8 NO EASY SURRENDER #185 Jan Mathews
- ___07802-6 IRRESISTIBLE YOU #186 Claudia Bishop
- ___07803-4 SURPRISED BY LOVE #187 Jasmine Craig
- ___07804-2 FLIGHTS OF FANCY #188 Linda Barlow
- ___07805-0 STARFIRE #189 Lee Williams
- ___07806-9 MOONLIGHT RHAPSODY #190 Kay Robbins
- ___07807-7 SPELLBOUND #191 Kate Nevins
- ___07808-5 LOVE THY NEIGHBOR #192 Frances Davies
- ___07809-3 LADY WITH A PAST #193 Elissa Curry
- ___07810-7 TOUCHED BY LIGHTNING #194 Helen Carter
- ___07811-5 NIGHT FLAME #195 Sarah Crewe
- ___07812-3 SOMETIMES A LADY #196 Jocelyn Day
- ___07813-1 COUNTRY PLEASURES #197 Lauren Fox
- ___07814-X TOO CLOSE FOR COMFORT #198 Liz Grady
- ___07815-8 KISSES INCOGNITO #199 Christa Merlin
- ___07816-6 HEAD OVER HEELS #200 Nicola Andrews
- ___07817-4 BRIEF ENCHANTMENT #201 Susanna Collins

All of the above titles are $1.95

Prices may be slightly higher in Canada.

Available at your local bookstore or return this form to:

SECOND CHANCE AT LOVE
Book Mailing Service
P.O. Box 690, Rockville Centre, NY 11571

Please send me the titles checked above. I enclose _____ Include 75¢ for postage and handling if one book is ordered; 25¢ per book for two or more not to exceed $1.75. California, Illinois, New York and Tennessee residents please add sales tax.

NAME_____

ADDRESS_____

CITY_____STATE/ZIP_____
(allow six weeks for delivery)   SK-41b

NEW FROM THE PUBLISHERS OF *SECOND CHANCE AT LOVE!*

To Have and to Hold™

	Title	Author	Code
___	THE TESTIMONY #1	Robin James	06928-0
___	A TASTE OF HEAVEN #2	Jennifer Rose	06929-9
___	TREAD SOFTLY #3	Ann Cristy	06930-2
___	THEY SAID IT WOULDN'T LAST #4	Elaine Tucker	06931-0
___	GILDED SPRING #5	Jenny Bates	06932-9
___	LEGAL AND TENDER #6	Candice Adams	06933-7
___	THE FAMILY PLAN #7	Nuria Wood	06934-5
___	HOLD FAST 'TIL DAWN #8	Mary Haskell	06935-3
___	HEART FULL OF RAINBOWS #9	Melanie Randolph	06936-1
___	I KNOW MY LOVE #10	Vivian Connolly	06937-X
___	KEYS TO THE HEART #11	Jennifer Rose	06938-8
___	STRANGE BEDFELLOWS #12	Elaine Tucker	06939-6
___	MOMENTS TO SHARE #13	Katherine Granger	06940-X
___	SUNBURST #14	Jeanne Grant	06941-8
___	WHATEVER IT TAKES #15	Cally Hughes	06942-6
___	LADY LAUGHING EYES #16	Lee Damon	06943-4
___	ALL THAT GLITTERS #17	Mary Haskell	06944-2
___	PLAYING FOR KEEPS #18	Elissa Curry	06945-0
___	PASSION'S GLOW #19	Marilyn Brian	06946-9
___	BETWEEN THE SHEETS #20	Tricia Adams	06947-7
___	MOONLIGHT AND MAGNOLIAS #21	Vivian Connolly	06948-5
___	A DELICATE BALANCE #22	Kate Wellington	06949-3
___	KISS ME, CAIT #23	Elissa Curry	07825-5
___	HOMECOMING #24	Ann Cristy	07826-3
___	TREASURE TO SHARE #25	Cally Hughes	07827-1
___	THAT CHAMPAGNE FEELING #26	Claudia Bishop	07828-X
___	KISSES SWEETER THAN WINE #27	Jennifer Rose	07829-8
___	TROUBLE IN PARADISE #28	Jeanne Grant	07830-1

All Titles are $1.95

Prices may be slightly higher in Canada.

Available at your local bookstore or return this form to:

SECOND CHANCE AT LOVE
Book Mailing Service
P.O. Box 690, Rockville Centre, NY 11571

Please send me the titles checked above. I enclose _____ Include 75¢ for postage and handling if one book is ordered; 25¢ per book for two or more not to exceed $1.75. California, Illinois, New York and Tennessee residents please add sales tax.

NAME_____

ADDRESS_____

CITY_____ STATE/ZIP_____

(allow six weeks for delivery)   THTH #67